Kadi

Thank

being one of the first to

support me. It truly means

a lot. I hope you enjoy

this trip through my old

stomping grounds.

Whiskey Road

a novel

Produced by Heidi Connolly
Harvard Girl Word Services at heidiconnolly.com

Whiskey Road

Shi Evans

Dedication

To Uncle Ronnie, whose face always lit up whenever he saw me. A visit didn't go by that you didn't tell me how smart and pretty I was— just what every little girl needs to hear. I miss you every day.

Acknowledgments

My family has kept me focused on my journey as a writer while completing Whiskey Road. I continue to be humbled by their unwavering support. Thank you, all.

Thanks also go to Lillard Evans, the Colonel. We're still together. Thank you for being there for me as I find my way through military life and for understanding my need to spread my wings since day one.

Savannah Evans—SavanTah (lip smack). Thank you for your unerring enthusiasm for everything I set out to accomplish...and especially for your daily question, "Mom, has anyone told you how pretty you look today?" You're my favorite daughter.

Noah Evans—My Noah, My Noah, My Noah. Thank you so much for thinking I'm cool enough to teach a creative writing class at your middle school and for not being too old to give me hugs and kisses every day. You're my favorite son.

Rosalyn Jackson—Mom, thank you for always being my number-one cheerleader, only one of the plethora of roles you've played in my life. I love you.

PART 1

Chapter 1

"Lillian, are you going to make me the happiest man alive and marry me?" Apparently, William Jameson, the current President of the United States of America, did not see his married status as a deterrent.

"I...." Lillian could not tear her eyes from the man she had loved since they had shared everything from grits to giggling with delight as they played endless games of hide-and-seek on the vast plantation.

And then, later, passion.

But it was not to be. Lillian asked God for strength. She would need it for the words she had to speak.

"I love you, Liam, I always have. Denver was my husband, and I loved him dearly, but you and I...we were different. You know that. But there is too much at stake."

"Mamma? Are you all right? Do you need to rest?"

Goldie turned to her daughter Shelby, who tended to cluck over her mamma like a mother hen.

"I'm fine," Goldie whispered, not wanting to interrupt Uncle Rich, really a family friend and not an uncle at all, who was storytelling. They all knew it was a capital offense to disrupt that man when he was deep into one of his stories. Unfortunately, this one about her mother Lillian was bringing back memories that Goldie ordinarily kept tucked away like the handkerchief in her sleeve.

Suddenly, all the celebrating felt forced and a lot less gay.

It was her seventy-seventh birthday. No one would be upset if someone of her age, the guest of honor, no less, required a bit of peace and quiet in between all the hubbub of celebration, would they? Uncle Rich's look of irritation aside, Goldie made it half way to the stairs before Shelby caught up to her. They'd both heard what was sure to be his next tale, too, one of his favorites, about how he'd outsmarted his boss during his sharecropping days, once too often.

They reached her daughter's guest bedroom, the perfect balance of designed serenity. Shelby had done well for herself, a beautiful home and a solid career in marketing, and Goldie was as proud as she could be. There was always a good time to be had by all here. Still, time apart was her favorite part of these gatherings.

"Hey, don't you think you can escape this soirée without me!" Rose, Goldie's younger sister, trailed them into the room.

"Mamma, something's wrong, isn't it? What aren't you telling me?" Shelby tut-tutted. "Come, lie down for a while. Let me get you a couple of throws."

Goldie obliged, feeling fine, but allowing Shelby to do what she needed to do.

"Are you excited to be returning home to Aiken, Mamma?"

When Goldie said nothing for a moment, Shelby sighed and turned to go. Her mother and she were powerfully close, but every once in a while, for as long as Shelby had known her, she'd had... moods. When they came on, it was best to let her be.

"No, don't leave, Shelby," Goldie protested. "Sit with me a while. You too, Rose. Come on over here and get under the covers."

Rose didn't need to be asked twice and snuggled in next to her sister.

Rose still marveled at how both of them had stayed so singularly well preserved, a testament to their good genes, really, since neither was a stranger to hard work and struggle. Why, just today a clerk at the store had commented that Rose Jackson Dupree didn't look a day over fifty-five! What with her silky chocolate skin with its rosy overtones and a complexion as flawless as her sister's, no one dared argue, either. When she was young she'd often worn her long shiny black hair tied up with ribbon. When she let it down for church, she professed to driving the young men wild. Today, a few gray strands framed her oval face, but she didn't let it stop her from adorning her still thick hair with the rhinestone barrettes her husband had sent her from South Korea during the war. She'd sure known how to bat her honey-brown eyes at him then, too, with lashes so thick she'd never had any need for mascara. Like many black families, the Jackson family was a hodgepodge of African and European descendants, which accounted for Goldie's honey-like skin and kinky light-brown hair with its natural blonde highlights as well.

Goldie pointed to a nearby chair for Shelby to pull next to the bed. "And to answer your question, Shelby, I'm not the least bit tired—physically, that is. And I am interested in seeing how much Aiken, South Carolina has changed," she said. "It's been a very, very long time."

"It sure has," said Rose. "But you know what they say, the more things change…."

"Truer words were never spoken," said Goldie, reaching out and holding Rose's hand. After all these years, they were still inseparable.

"Do you think your old house is still there, Mamma?"

"So I've heard. I talked to my old friend Bertha and she said a small family lives there now. Sadly, she said it's seen better days.

All this talk about Aiken has me thinking about our other home, though."

"What other home?" asked Shelby. She'd never heard mention of any other family home.

"The one in Virginia," said Rose.

"What do you mean, the one in Virginia?" Shelby smarted. "I've never heard about any house in Virginia."

"That's because we never told you about it," said Goldie. "But I think maybe I should. Rose?"

"I say it's about time!"

Shelby looked at the women she thought she knew. What were they up to? "Well, then, hurry up," she said, "and don't leave out any of the good stuff. Especially about Mamma, Aunt Rose. What was she really like back then?"

"You want to know what your Mamma was like," said Rose, "then we have to start way back in Aiken...and such a beautiful town it was."

"Amen to that," murmured Goldie, already back on Aiken's infamous Whiskey Road, feeling the dirt beneath her feet.

Chapter 2

The Jackson sisters were well known for their beauty. Even in their baby carriages they drew the attention of passersby. Of course, during their growing-up years, Rose and Goldie thought only about leaving Aiken, South Carolina, which they saw as nothing more than a hick town with fewer opportunities than old Mr. Clem had teeth. If you weren't white, and didn't have the money that went with that privilege, your house was most likely on the wrong side of the tracks, and the only way you stepped foot into the private clubs where they played golf and polo was if you worked there. It seemed the only way to appreciate the virtues of Aiken was to leave it.

The coastal town, planned in the early 1830s by two engineers who worked for one of the railroad companies constructing a railroad to connect Charleston, was part of South Carolina's low country. Aiken, named after Governor William Aiken, Sr., of Charleston—who just happened to be president of the railroad—was the railroad's terminus, and the planners had instituted a grid street plan for the city. Initially, the railroad ran down Park Avenue, dividing the town exactly in two. This route caused a problem, however, because the trains had to travel a steep incline. To fix this hardship, a thirty-foot-deep cut was dug, one which essentially completed the town's division in more ways than one into the north side and the south side. If you visit Aiken today, several bridges still stand connecting the north to the south, but back then the cut was a line of demarcation, and blacks—or the colored, as they were called, along with a number of other not-so-nice terms—were not allowed past it after dark.

In truth, only one train passed through Aiken. They called this train the Best Friend as it brought in commerce and tourists who needed accommodations and food. Aiken made a concerted effort to keep hotels filled all year round by advertising its offerings of a warm climate and resort status to northerners.

"It was the early 1930s," started Rose. "Business was concentrated around Laurens Street and Richland Avenue, an area known as Uptown Aiken. And then there was Downtown Aiken, around, around . . . what was that street called, Goldie?"

"Park Avenue, Rose. It's not like Aiken had that many streets." Even though Goldie was the oldest, she felt she had the better memory of the two and liked to show it off.

Rose chose to ignore the jibe this time. "Yes, that's right, Park Avenue and York Street. The funny thing was there were only a few streets between Uptown and Downtown Aiken, but I guess calling them that made Aiken sound bigger than it really was."

Rose shook her head, but smiled. "They built the city around this grid pattern, which made it favorable to traffic and business. You know, back then it wasn't as easy for cars to go in reverse, and the grid pattern made driving a little easier. There were beautiful parks, too, right in the middle of commerce areas, with immaculately landscaped medians. Aiken never had as many parks as Savannah, Georgia, of course, but they fit our fair city just as well."

"It was our daddy who was responsible for the upkeep of two of those parks," Goldie interrupted proudly. "They were filled with exotic trees, flowers, and shrubs. Oh, it was an elegant place, Shelby, and that wasn't all that attracted the wealthy to Aiken."

"Sounds like Aiken was a rich town, huh, Mamma?"

"Oh, yes—rich with blue bloods and prosperity, that is. For some, it became known as a refuge for those seeking relief from malaria along the coast. Back then they thought it was caused by the swamp air, you know. But once they got to Aiken, they fell in love with it and stayed."

"There was plenty of money, that's for sure," Rose agreed. "And the mansions! My, oh my. Each one representing the folk's standing and pedigree back home." Rose tapped her nose. "Let's see. There were those whose money came from horse breeding and those whose money came from liquor or farming or industry. They all loved to vacation in Aiken and escape the cold and snow up north, mostly staying at the Wilbridge Inn, still in operation today."

"'Cept blacks are welcome now, Rose, there's the difference," said Goldie.

"True enough. Though I don't know if anything's changed over at the Blue Landing Club."

The sisters paused to consider the question, but the answer eluded them.

"While vacationing they had to have something to do, of course," said Goldie. "So, they brought their a-ris-to-cra-tic sports." The class system of the old south still made Goldie boil. "That's how polo and golf flourished in those parts." Amazingly, their small town of Aiken had become the polo center of the world and had even joined the United States Polo Association as its tenth member, and their very own Whitney Field boasted a record or two on the books as a result.

"The mild climate was perfect for polo," she continued, "and just what the horses needed. In fact, many horse trainers congregated in Aiken to tone their steeds for spring races. That's why the Thoroughbred Racing Hall of Fame is located there. In fact, Aiken still hosts the Triple Crown, which takes up three weekends on the city's calendar. One weekend for harness racing, one for the Aiken Trials, and the last for the Aiken Steeplechase. Course, we weren't allowed to participate in the sport, but we got to watch the races with our families—from a different section, of course." As far back as 1893 the elite whites formed clubs where the only coloreds who entered were the servants.

"We sure did think we were something else," Rose reminisced. "All dressed up like the white folks, our own social scene going on. I didn't care what anybody said, either," she harrumphed. "We all knew they were looking over to see what we were wearing and how nice we looked."

Goldie gave Rose a high-five. "That's right. But polo and the Triple Crown weren't the only sporting events that attracted the wealthy to Aiken. Golf was as popular as the horses."

Rose's interest in golf was about as high as her interest in going to the dentist. "We didn't participate much at the golf matches, though," she said. "That sure is one boring-ass sport."

"Aunt Rose!" Shelby laughed, but Aunt Rose just shook her head.

Rose continued her tour of Aiken. "Going west on South Boundary Street, you went through what appeared to be a tunnel, where magnificent oak trees on both sides of the road leaned over to meet each other as if they were playing the London Bridge game. You remember, Shelby. You used to play it with your friends when you were little." Shelby nodded. "The mantles of gray-green moss draped the trees and made for the loveliest shade on all those hot days. But some days the tunnel felt downright eerie, right Goldie?"

"It sure did. But then other times it almost felt romantic."

Rose pictured it. "I used to dream that I'd ride down that road in a horse-drawn carriage on my wedding day," she said. "I didn't get that lucky, of course, but it sort of felt like the same idea at my military wedding when I walked down between the rows of soldiers with their swords drawn. Maybe that's why I wanted to marry an army officer." The far-away look in her eyes was a clear sign that she was thinking about her beloved husband who'd passed so long ago.

Goldie put her arm around Rose and gave her a squeeze.

"You see, Shelby," she said, "South Carolina State University not only offered wonderful educational opportunities to young blacks, it gave the young men the chance to receive a commission into the United States Army. The program began in 1947. The commissions were mostly in the support area, but nonetheless paved the way for all blacks today. In fact, South Carolina State has commissioned more blacks than any other college or university. At least ten generals hail from SCSU. Rose's husband was an important part of that history."

"How do you know so much about military history, Mamma?"

Goldie laughed. "Your Aunt Rose won't let me forget, that's how. And that's how your Uncle Dan got his commission."

"But didn't you graduate from South Carolina State in the late 1930s, Aunt Rose? I thought you and Uncle Dan were the same age."

"Dan went to college a little later than most of the rest of us, honey, because of his time in the army," Rose said quietly.

There was a moment of respectful reflection. Then Goldie said, "But that tunnel of oaks sure was special. And even on our side of town the flowers and trees grew, whether the city officials planned it or not. From their perspective, why waste resources if the wealthier white residents and tourists would be staying on their side of town? Guess that vegetation had a mind of its own.

"They called the well-to-do black part of Aiken, on the north side, Washington Circle. Mostly small business owners, teachers, laborers, and the like lived there in modest three- or four-bedroom homes with attractive landscaped yards. The Freeman family owned the general store there. Farther out on the north side? That was called Shiloh Heights. A lot of farmers lived there. Some of the poorest blacks lived in those woods past Shiloh Heights, right along with some of the poorest whites. The situation was a tinderbox just waiting to be lit."

Well-off or poor, Aiken's blacks had two things in common: surviving the often oppressive southern lack of hospitality and their reliance on the church. They met in homes, in barns, anywhere you could think of to meet up and pray. Churches were a lot more than just buildings, serving as pillars of stability, growth, and certainty to the entire community. Churches were places where people came together for comfort as well as decision making and planning, say, for example, when local hate groups got it in their heads to perpetrate violence. Time and again, people went back to their drawing board, their churches, to find a sense of stability, to raise the needed funds for whatever family was in need.

Goldie knew that one of Aiken's black churches, founded in 1865, was still serving the community of Aiken. Initially when blacks were invited to join the Aiken Baptist Church they were required to sit in a separate section from the whites. After a riot in nearby Ellenton, many more African Americans relocated to Aiken and joined Aiken Baptist. Eventually, when they began to outnumber the whites, a new meeting house became necessary. The new congregation moved into a brand new building and called themselves the African Baptist Church. After a fire destroyed that structure, another church, designed by a white Civil War hero, was built on the same spot.

Over the years, the church, boasting one of the largest memberships in Aiken, had sponsored various community programs and projects. Lillian, Goldie and Rose's mother, was married in African Baptist, had confirmed her babies there, and buried her husband there after his lynching at the hands of one of Aiken's more "prestigious" groups of men.

Aiken Baptist Church of Aiken stayed on, however, becoming as important to the white residents of Aiken, including Mayor Stanton and Sheriff Baker, who were avid church-goers and took as much pride in their faith as anyone. In the middle of Aiken on the edge of the south side, Aiken Baptist was a beautiful structure worthy of its parishioners who possessed elegance, grace, and refinement. They were especially proud of their colored membership and maintained a special section in the sanctuary just for them.

Chapter 3

When Rose and Goldie were growing up, the tall brick walls of Aiken protected immaculate lawns and stately manors where the white elite met to discuss ways to maintain their standing, protect their heritage, and preserve what was "rightfully theirs as handed down by the hand of God." Behind the majestic magnolia trees and grand oak trees with Spanish moss to cool the hot humid temperatures, Aiken's well-to-do strategized about how to keep the coloreds from getting too uppity and expecting more rights. The privileged class was much too well bred to get their hands muddy by dealing directly with black individuals, however. That was the job of the various local hate groups.

South Carolina as a state did not stray from the party line of suppressing freedom for blacks either. Pushed to recognize the end to slavery, it quickly imposed stringent economic and social restrictions on former slaves. Black farmers required written permission from an employer or judge to sell their products, for example, and weapons were expressly forbidden in case retaliation became a possibility. A black person might find him- or herself arrested at the drop of a hat if a white person determined an infraction had been committed, and a "sunrise to sunset" law kept their movements under the direct scrutiny of law enforcement in the name of so-called Black Codes.

African Americans were limited in their professions, of course, mostly permitted to earn meager livings as farm laborers, day laborers, or hired servants. Sure, being free men and women able to make a living wage sounded a lot better than being a slave, but in South Carolina, at least, it wasn't much of an improvement. There were all sorts of reasons for having one's pay docked, for example. If you left work without the supervisor's permission, let's say, or you "caused" the employer's equipment to show wear and tear. Too sick to work? They docked your pay. Lazy? They docked your pay. Talked during your shift? They docked your pay. And nothing, but nothing, could stop the beatings at the hands of the ones in power.

Generally speaking, blacks felt no safer "free" than they did under the rule of slavery. Ironically, slavery had provided a semblance of protection. You would think common sense would prevent someone from destroying his investment. But sadly, for many slaves, such logic would not save them and with emancipation came the maiming and lynching that remained part of their daily lives.

Naturally, the South Carolina legislature had a vested interest in keeping blacks as close to slaves as legally possible. Without legal protection, there would be no relief at hand, either, not in the courts where rulings favored whites, no matter the dispute or on the streets. Plantation owners were encouraged to detain laborers who "owed them money" from various pay dockings as well. Hence, economic opportunity for blacks was nonexistent; that is, until they were beckoned northward by the promise of higher standards and opportunity.

South Carolina had its share of industrial plants that depended on cheap labor to ensure productivity, too. Blacks worked for menial pay and under harsh plantation conditions, which only differed in how bad they were depending on the plant. It was when the lynching reached mammoth proportions that many blacks decided to take a chance and migrate north to escape the fear, intimidation, and violence. It is believed that approximately 700,000 blacks ultimately left the south for northern lands. When they did, much of the local industrial workforce was depleted.

The state of South Carolina had one of the highest rankings of any state for black lynchings, no surprise given the plethora of white supremacist groups with names like the Pale Faces, Sons of Midnight, and the Knights of the White Camelia. Lillian Ruth Taylor, mother of Goldie and Ruth Jackson, herself always said the most notorious of them all was the World of the White Order.

Fortunately for the Jackson girls, Lillian Ruth Taylor was there to guide them through the worst of it. Lillian Taylor had moved to Aiken in the early 1900s when the Black Codes were in full effect. She admonished the girls many times not to let the sun go down on them if they happened to be on the south side of Aiken Township. Again, without a special permit from their employer or one signed by a judge, being on the wrong side of town after sunset would leave them open for all manner of beating or even arrest by the authorities.

Under the World of the White Order's first grand leader supreme, Cannon T. Wood, aka "The Hatchet," the WWO quickly spread across the south. Some say Wood was responsible for the massacre of African American troops as they tried to surrender during the Civil War. Apparently, Wood himself gave the signal for the troops to place their weapons on the ground and then walked straight up to their commander and shot him point blank in the head as the soldier held his hands in the air. Then, when the rest of the soldiers scattered to escape their impending fate, Wood gave the order for his men to open fire, at which point most of the soldiers were shot in the back or the back of the head.

"'See these cowards,'" Lillian used to say, shaking her head and quoting Wood, "'They couldn't even turn around and take their bullets like honorable men. I am disgusted to have to fight dishonorable men. They are unworthy to stand on the same field as me. That's what they get for listening to the lies told to them by scumbag northerners. These niggers' blood rests on their hands, not mine. They should know better than to think they can beat any man of the white race. Hear this, f---ing niggers!—' "Excuse me, Lord,"— 'Stepping out of line is stepping into the woods. You don't want to enter the woods, because that's where you'll find me, waiting under my hood.'"

As the WWO spread across the south, so did the violence and terror perpetrated by the other hate groups. At one point, their activity in South Carolina became so prevalent that many outsiders were left to wonder how such cruelties could flourish amid the fine "moral sense" cultivated in the state's white communities. How could such atrocities happen right under the noses of those who were supposedly so civilized, so cultured, so genteel?

It may not come as a surprise that economics, not morality, was what turned the tide. Or that soon thereafter the southern industrialists were pressuring the government to crack down on the killings and mob violence that was terrorizing its valuable cheap workforce, specifically in the industry where cotton was king.

Top heavy with privileged whites, Aiken recognized its need for willing workers to toe the line in the filthy industrial plants. Still, although the lynchings slowed, the intimidation and lack of possible advancement for blacks remained. The attempt to vote, to attend better schools, to strive for a better standard of living...all were met with burning crosses and radical acts that said NO, and southern "justice" continued unabated.

Chapter 4

Denver Jackson, Lillian Taylor's husband, had never been one to adhere to the status quo. In his position as owner of his own landscaping business, he had plans to expand his business to neighboring Augusta, Georgia, an act which would surely ruffle many a white feather.

"Daddy said that if only he could expand into Augusta, we'd have a much bigger house on Washington Circle," Rose told Shelby. "Maybe even on Easy Street."

Easy Street sat off Whiskey Road about one-eighth of a mile at the point where it changed from Chesterfield Street. Technically, it was not condoned for blacks to live on the south side of Aiken, but they were permitted on Easy Street due to its proximity to the houses of the wealthy whites in which they worked. Because Denver Jackson was one of the blacks who worked in that capacity, it was the perfect location for his family.

"We had a three-bedroom house," said Rose. "Sure, it was plain, but it was ours. I can still see it. Not much as far as exterior ornamentation goes, but it was cute as a button, green with white shutters on the two windows that framed the front door. The roof was steep, with side gables and a small overhang. Mamma kept flowers on each window sill, which made the porch smell so nice in the spring. We even had an attic that helped with the living space, and luxurious hardwood floors." She could see her old home clear as day. "My daddy, your granddaddy, Shelby, Denver Jackson, worked hard every day to provide that home for us."

Rose's eyes dulled with the ache of the past. She shook her head. "Poor Daddy. Lynched like that...." She pulled out a handkerchief and dabbed at her eyes. "My my, even after all these years, it still hurts. Poor man, mistaken for another and taking the blame. All over some other man who'd had an affair with a married white woman."

Shelby gaped, afraid to breathe. This was the first time she'd hear the details of her granddaddy's death and she didn't want anything to get in the way of the telling.

"I was only twelve years old at the time," Rose went on in that same sad voice. "And Goldie here was just thirteen. But even we knew the truth. That Cora Bidenfield identified the wrong man to protect her lover. Even though everyone knew Daddy was madly in love with Mamma and would never ever have stepped out on her."

"They were in love, that's for certain," said Goldie, sniffling as well. "'Course, back then all that smooching set us to giggling and hiding, didn't it, Rose?"

"That's a fact, Goldie," said Rose, "that's a fact," picking up a tissue to wipe her eyes.

"Our Mamma served Daddy coffee and breakfast every day," said Goldie, "every day of their lives, that is, until his death."

. . .

"Mornin', baby."
"Mornin', sweetie."

Denver reached over for his morning embrace, but didn't linger. "Don't have much time this morning, so I'll just...."

"You know what's good for you," Lillian said, "you'll sit down and eat. After I done worked so hard in this kitchen making you and the girls breakfast...."

"All right, all right." Denver knew when he was licked. "But I sure like it when you get all bossy."

The girls giggled behind their hands, adoring their parents and the love they shared, though they'd never admit it out loud.

Lillian set down a plate stacked high with flapjacks and maple syrup, a side of country ham and bacon, and jelly toast in front of her man. The girls got ham and two flapjacks a piece, since they claimed they were now watching their figures.

Something on Denver's face caused a crease to appear in Lillian's forehead. "Is there something I need to know, Denver?"

Goldie and Rose felt their stomachs knot at their father's sudden mood change, one which had been increasingly touchy over the past few days. Their daddy was usually a loving, attentive man who loved a good joke. But he often had his hands in the community affairs of his people, and that meant dealing with the law and the WWO.

For instance, when John Chavious got picked up by the sheriff's office one night for public drunkenness, it was Denver who went straight to Sheriff Baker and negotiated a way for Chavious to pay his fine in installments so he could continue to make a living and support his pregnant wife, Pearl, a friend of Lillian's. As usual, Sheriff Baker was willing to help. Especially since it meant Chavious would make two extra payments that would go straight into Baker's personal till.

Denver knew he was playing with fire, of course, because Sheriff "Bull" Baker was himself a high-ranking member of the WWO. Still, over the years the sheriff and he had established a sort of mutual respect out of necessity. When Denver said Bull would get his money, he always got it, even if it had to come from Denver's own pocket to cover another man's debt. And Denver could be sure that Bull's word was good, that freedom could be had for the extra fees imposed without retaliation from certain factions. Bull's word, like Denver's, had always been as good as gold.

Unfortunately, this time was different. A white woman's good name was at stake, and Sheriff Bull Baker was smack in the middle of the latest scandal.

Cora Bidenfield. Now, hers was a name that brought shame to whites and fodder to blacks. Over time, poking fun at Cora Bidenfield had become one of the small ways that blacks could rise above the lot they'd been assigned by the whites.

Cora Bidenfield was well known in Aiken for her predilection for messing around with black men. In fact, her family's standing in the community was the only thing that kept her in the town's relative good graces. Perhaps if times were different she might have taken the long walk to the north side of Aiken, even tied the knot with a black man, but not now. Not in these times, and not in Aiken, South Carolina.

And not with the married man she had set her sights on, the one for whom all the others were substitutes: Denver Jackson.

Cora had first laid eyes on Denver when they were children and he'd come to her house with his father, who owned a landscaping business, to work on their yard. Instead of sharecropping land in the traditional sense, David Jackson had borrowed tools enough to start his own business, paid off his debt over time, and took his boys along to teach them the trade. His most important objective, however, was to teach them to earn an honest living and deal with the white people they'd serve.

The boys needed to know which white people wanted their yards worked by ghosts—who had no contact with the owners—

and which ones were friendly-like and expected a little conversation. Which ones would call them boys, niggers, or, even, occasionally, one of the family. Sometimes they'd be called all three by different members of the same family, a confusing reality. If a client praised their work, they needed to know just how to respond to keep up the politic politeness. So, when Mr. Jacobs said, "You are the best yard boy in the state of South Carolina, David," David Jackson's carefully modulated response was always, "Oh, no suh, Mr. Jacobs, it ain't me. You just bought the best grass seed and flowers money could buy." Though David Jackson had no formal education, he and his family read anything they could get their hands on. When they talked to white people, however, the most important thing was not to sound too smart or intelligent or be considered "uppity." Soon, David Jackson had changed his response to "Oh, no sir, Mr. Cannon, it isn't I. You have the best seed and flowers, only makes my job look easy," but made sure that response came with hooded downcast eyes.

Knowing how to talk to white people was a skill Denver Jackson learned early, therefore, a skill that helped in his dealings with Bull Baker and the WWO. Never did he expect it would help with the likes of Cora Jacobs Bidenfield. But it took a bit of tricky maneuvering to ward off her advances and reject all that pushy womanhood. It was his job to convince her that it was he, not she, who was being rejected, or face a wrath that no man would relish.

Ultimately, however, Denver's gentle, persistent letdowns were too much for Cora to bear, and only incited her to want him all the more.

Sure, there were some black men who, unlike Denver, were willing to put all risk aside for the pleasures of the flesh. Carl Wright was one such unlucky man. It was only two weeks before that Cora's husband pulled up into their yard just as she and Carl had finished some steamy business of their own.

Though Cora attempted to cover for Carl as he crept out the back door, her suspicious behavior had John at the window quick as a minute, where he spied some fool hoofing it down the driveway on foot. In a hot minute he was through the door and slapping Cora's face. "Which nigger was that I just saw hauling ass down my driveway on foot, woman?! You tell me, Cora, you tell me right now, so as I can have his balls strung up from a tree!"

"I don't know," Cora sobbed, praying to strum up a respectable enough stream of tears for the occasion.

"Don't you lie to me, Cora. I told you if this ever happened again I would kill the sonovabitch who came near my wife!"

"John," Cora wailed, "just let it go. Please. If you let this one go, I promise it'll never happen again."

They both knew she was lying.

"Either tell me who he was," John warned, "or I'll be seeing you in divorce court, you hear me?"

They both knew Cora would never let that happen, either.

"John, I said I promise. It'll never happen again. Please don't make a big stink about this. If you say anything about divorce, people will talk. They'll know why."

John's eyes suddenly took on the look of a fox.

"Oh no, they won't. We'll just tell them what really happened. That my poor wife was victimized. Raped. By a highfalutin' nigger."

Cora's tears dried up so fast you might wonder if they'd ever been there in the first place. "What? But John, you can't! They'll... they'll kill him."

"You got that right."

Cora's head spun. She had to think of something. Anything. She couldn't let anything happen to the man. But what else could she do? The distance between the rock and a hard place widened.

"I'll...I'll tell you, then. If I have to."

John put the arm he'd again raised down. "Well? I'm waiting."

"It was…it was…Denver Jackson."

"Denver Jackson? My, oh my, Cora, you think I'm plum crazy or something? I know that sonovabitch wasn't Denver Jackson." He looked at her, but Cora said nothing.

"All right, all right. If that's the way you want to play it, we'll let it slide for the moment, see how far you're willing to take this thing." John paused for effect. "Whether you're willing to let an innocent man die."

Cora remained silent holding her cheek where her husband had hit her.

"All righty, then," said John, shaking his head, "I'll just take myself off to talk to Sheriff Baker."

John Bidenfield was powerfully disappointed in his wife. The rumors of her affairs were legendary by now; although emasculating, the constant elbow ribbing he got around town had gotten old and few were willing to take on John after a drink or two. But Cora's "admission" was plain old sad. Denver Jackson was a good man. A man who worked for many of the prominent families of Aiken. Cora knew what she was doing when she'd named him, and if it was like a kick in the gut for John, no telling how it would feel to the black community.

However, the scandal of a divorce was not a possibility, not for the Bidenfield clan. With their name at stake, his only option was to make an example of Jackson, to let all the other coloreds know what would happen if they messed with Cora or any other white woman. Five minutes later he was in the sheriff's office.

. . .

"Bull, I need to report a crime."

"Well, hello to you, too, John."

"I'm serious, Bull. Cora's been raped. By a nigger."

Bull, who had been tipped back in his chair, leaned forward and the legs crashed to the floor. "Raped? Cora?" He gave John a hard look. "You real sure about that, John?"

"What the hell kind of question is that, Bull? I just told you some sonovabitch raped Cora, and you ask me if I'm sure?" John knew his righteous indignation sounded puny, but it was the best he could do.

"Well, John," said the sheriff, stalling for time to find a way to put delicately what he needed to say, "it's just that, well, you know, Cora's not exactly been the pillar of…of…" he searched for the right word "…decorum the last few years. And you know the talk—"

"I don't give a damn what kind of talk you all have heard," John said loudly. "I'm telling you Cora was raped. That's all you need to know."

"Okay, John, okay. Relax, okay? Why don't you sit down and tell me about it?"

John proceeded to share the lie he'd concocted on his way to the station. When he pointed a finger at Denver Jackson, Bull was incredulous.

"Denver Jackson? I don't believe it."

"Well, you'd better believe it. You know Denver's cousin works for us. He must have told Denver all the help had the day off. Wouldn't be hard to show up pretending he was supposed to work on the grounds today. Poor gullible Cora would have accepted that story without a thought."

Bull looked keenly at John, but John wouldn't meet his eye.

"Why would Cora give the help the day off?" Bull asked. John's story had more holes than a piece of Swiss cheese.

"You know how touchy Cora is, Bull. Sometimes she needs a bit of space to, um, collect herself without all the help around." John looked somewhere over Bull's head, out the window, anywhere but at the sheriff.

"Right," said Bull.

Bull was in a quandary. Some other man in his position might be salivating at the prospect of dealing with a nigger who'd gone astray. But not Bull. And not if it were Denver Jackson. "You say you found this character in Cora's bed, John? You telling me he took the time to take Cora to the bedroom 'fore he did his business?"

John pounded his fist on Bull's desk. "Look Bull, I'm not going to tell you again. Cora was having one of her spells. Likely as not, she was probably already in the bed when he got there."

Bull put up his hands. "Okay, okay," he said. "Take it easy, John. Let me think, all right?"

John waited unhappily until Bull spoke again. "See here, now, John. You know any black man even looks in Cora's direction—or any of our women—I'd be all over him. But pointing the finger at Denver Jackson? Well, that gives me cause to pause."

The sheriff was keenly aware that he was in a precarious position. He had recently been given marching orders by Mayor Zachary Stanton to keep things quiet in the city. If anything happened to Denver over this supposed "rape" they could have an uprising on their hands. His people might tolerate Cora Bidenfield's accusing some knucklehead, but not Denver Jackson. He was the one they relied on to be their spokesperson, their liaison to the whites. He was black as any of them, of course, but Bull couldn't help but feel respect for the way Denver handled his affairs. Not that Bull'd be shouting it from the rooftops any time soon.

"I know you're not saying you don't believe me," John said, the threat deep in his voice.

"Naw, naw, I'm not saying that," Bull backpedaled. Bidenfield support could make or break his chances for reelection. He had to play this one very carefully. "I'm just saying I know Denver, and that doesn't sound like him. Maybe Cora…is it possible that she might be protecting some other guy?"

"Bull, I'm telling you one last time. Cora said what she said, that Denver Jackson raped her. And he has to pay for it."

Bull sighed. "Okay, John. I hear you. But, 'fore we take this any further, do me a big favor? Go back to Cora. Talk to her when you're not so upset. Maybe she's just scared to tell you who it really was, or what really happened." Bull raised his eyebrows and said called up as much diplomacy as he could muster. "'Cause you and me both know it is highly unlikely that Denver Jackson was the man who done this thing. And if I have to bring in Denver Jackson and let you all do what's fit and proper for such a crime, we're gonna have a lot more bloodshed than that on our hands."

Would John take the carrot? wondered Bull. The man was as, if not more, politically connected than most wealthy white men in Aiken. Bloodshed wasn't the problem. It was pacifying Zachary Stanton, who was about to become senator. As long as Bull kept things quiet and orderly, he'd be feeling the gratitude down the line.

"All right, I'll talk to Cora again," John finally agreed. "But I'm not promising anything."

Bull let out a long breath, praying the whole thing would up and go away.

Chapter 5

Denver's wife Lillian was afraid.

The problem wasn't standing by her man. She'd do anything she had to do to protect the man she loved, the man she knew was innocent. The problem was whether justice would be served.

"There's no way around it," said Denver. "I have to go see Bull about this...this situation."

Goldie and Rose stood nearby, for the first time in their lives unsure about what their parents' behavior meant. Their arguing the night before was unusual and disturbing, about how they'd handle this so-called "situation."

"Rose, Goldie, off to school or you'll be late," Lillian called. The girls came around the corner and sheepishly took their food packets from their mother's hand.

"Yes, Mamma," said Goldie, understanding her mother was in no mood this morning for lollygagging about. She and Rose got their things together without any of the usual halfhearted backtalk.

Denver kissed his girls on the cheek with tenderness. "You girls have a good day at school, hear?"

"Yes, Daddy."

When the girls were gone there was no more delaying what needed to be said. "Denver," said Lillian, "you need to tell Bull that he needs to question Cora directly, and I mean put the fear of God in her, make that woman tell the truth."

"Babe, don't you think I want my name cleared more than anyone?" Denver's normally animated face was dejected. "I know what's at stake."

"That's why you need to talk to Bull again instead of waiting on Cora to come to her senses. Not that that woman has any."

"Darn it, Lillian, what do you want me to do? Beg? What about my pride?"

"Damn that pride of yours, Denver. We are talking about your life. Our lives."

Denver was shocked. Lillian rarely cursed, believing those who cursed only did so because they were unable to express themselves properly. He made up his mind. "All right, Lillian. I'll go plead my case."

"If it doesn't work, we will simply have to go somewhere else, Denver. Leave Aiken altogether. We can't be living under this cloud."

Denver stopped. "That I'll never do, Lillian. I was born in Aiken, and I will die in Aiken. This here is where home is. I won't run like a coward," he declared. "Curse all you want to, but I just won't do it. Not even for you."

Denver left Lillian speechless, his unfinished breakfast on the table, to go see the sheriff.

. . .

Lillian washed up the breakfast dishes with a heavy heart. She asked the Lord to forgive her for cursing, in the same breath praying for him to spare her husband. Her innocent, kind husband who'd

38

never hurt anyone in his life. The more she washed, the more angry Lillian became, until finally she hurled the pie plate in her soapy hands at the wall, smashing it into a million pieces. Life without her man, she thought, the tears streaming down her cheeks, was unthinkable.

As a young woman, Lillian had moved to Aiken to live with her Aunt Jean. Though not a blood relative, Jean was a good family friend who had quickly become like a second mother to her charge. Not long after the move Lillian had met Denver Jackson. Before that, she, her mother Eloise, and her sister had lived in Virginia, on the Jameson plantation. On the outside, the Jameson plantation was one of the wealthiest in the country, producing cotton and tobacco. But on the inside, the generations were busy producing a lot more in the form of one William Jameson, heir apparent, who was being groomed for the White House. Everyone agreed he had the makings of a fine president and that nothing could stop William Jameson's trajectory toward the highest office in the country.

Nothing, that is, except, perhaps, Lillian. "Liam" and "Elle," as William liked to call her, grew up together. Born only a few days apart on the plantation, they spent most every day of their childhoods together, either in the Jameson kitchen, where Eloise worked, or outside on the plantation grounds. Eloise ran her kitchen with a stern hand, and directed all events inside the house as well, what with Liam's mother too busy with parties and outings to concern herself with housekeeping matters or the children's whereabouts.

Eloise adored Liam, and he worshipped her right back. When school and lessons were done for the day, Liam could always be found at Eloise's side, right next to Elle. Liam was a natural-born teacher, teaching Elle just about everything he learned. He helped her fine-tune her reading, lending her all the classics, and helped her with all her other studies, too.

It didn't take long before Liam began to appreciate Elle for the lovely young woman she was growing up to be. With the devilish twinkle in Liam's eye that made all the girls melt and his million-dollar smile, Elle was not immune to his charms either. By the time they were adolescents, they had eyes only for each other.

Their conversation covered all sorts of topics, including controversial ones like equal rights. Fortunately, they never wanted for privacy, with all the acreage of the plantation available to them. Their favorite place was a small cabin by a large pond that Liam's father used when he felt the need for a little time with his buddies, fishing or hunting or just plain tossing back a few and smoking a good cigar.

"Elle, when I become president, I am going to change this country," Liam told Lillian confidently as they sat on the porch of the cabin in the shade.

Lillian snorted. "Liam, it's gonna take more than your dreams to change this country."

"Come on, Elle, don't you have faith in me?"

"Sure I do, Liam. It ain't you I don't have faith in."

"Ain't?"

"Isn't, then." Lillian rolled her eyes. She didn't like to be corrected, but she tolerated it from Liam. "It's your friends and colleagues I'm worried about. Everybody is not like you, Liam."

"Well, everybody can't be lucky enough to be like me, I guess," said Liam with a grin.

"And a good thing, too," said Lillian. "This world can't possibly handle two Liams. The girls would lose their minds."

Liam reached out for Lillian. He'd made similar overtures before, but this time, when she didn't resist, he put his arms around her waist and pulled her closer. Her arms naturally circled his broad shoulders.

"How about you, Elle? Are you losing your mind right about now?"

Lillian had been in Liam's close proximity her entire life. But this was different. And she'd never ever been so near to a man before, let alone the most handsome man around and the future President of the United States.

Liam was the perfect fit for Lillian's own size and shape. A few inches taller than she, she looked up into his chiseled face with its frame of dark curls. The feel of his muscular build against her lithe smooth body had her quivering with desire. The thought drew her attention to something else as well. Liam was aroused! She was shocked, but prideful at the same time to think she had caused it.

"You are so beautiful, Elle," said Liam, his voice husky and rough. Liam knew he had a reputation. He flirted with other girls all the time—and liked the attention—but he'd been holding out for Lillian for as long as he could remember.

"You are, too, Liam."

"Me?" Liam smiled as if she'd said something funny.

Lillian was embarrassed. She was new to all this. She'd certainly never had a boyfriend, or even been kissed. "You know what I mean," she said, and gave him a little push, but he drew her back to him.

"I know how I feel about you, Elle. I can't wait to see you when we're apart. I think about you all the time. And you must know not all my thoughts are pure. In fact, I'd say they're downright naughty sometimes."

He planted a kiss on Lillian's forehead. The sensation prickled from her scalp all the way down to her toes. Would he kiss her lips? Would he dare? Would she let him?

"Oh, really?" she asked nonchalantly, or so she hoped, as if the flame in her face would not give her away.

"Yes, that's right. I think about kissing you all over, Elle, and sure would like to explore a lot more than your forehead."

Lillian's reaction, she knew, was thoroughly unladylike. The bells in her head were going off the way church bells did on Sunday mornings. But she didn't care. All she wanted, all she could think about, was Liam.

"Elle? Where did you go? Did you hear what I just said?"

"Oh! Yes, Liam. It's just that I was just...I was just—" Suddenly, Lillian could say no more. She placed her hands around Liam's neck and drew his lips to hers.

Liam gasped in surprise, responded without hesitation in kind, and was lost. The world outside them ceased to exist.

. . .

When Liam raised her dress over her hips so he could put his hands on her body, Lillian had let him, realizing that no man had ever seen her undergarments before. For a moment, she was ashamed of their bleached, plain whiteness. Then she saw the heat in Liam's eyes and knew they didn't matter a whit.

"Why are you looking at me like that?" Lillian asked, knowing full well why because she was feeling the same way. She felt so beautiful that for a second she forgot she was the daughter of a poor maid and a sharecropper.

Suddenly, Liam backed away.

Horrified, instantly remorseful and full of doubt, Lillian went to cover up, ashamed.

"No," said Liam. "Stop. You're beautiful. It's just that—wait. I'll show you."

Lillian waited uncomfortably, sure Liam had changed his mind about her, as he stepped inside the cabin, rummaged around inside, then returned.

When he came out he was holding something in his hand. "Here," he said. "I hope you like it."

Surprised, Lillian asked, "What is it?"

"Open it, silly. See for yourself."

"All right." Lillian sat back down on the step and looked at the box. She'd never gotten a present before, least not from anyone not related to her. Even the bow on the box was gorgeous, a luxurious lavender satin bow she vowed to save forever.

Gingerly she removed the lid and set it beside her, while Liam, flushed with need, perched on the stair below. Slowly she folded aside the paper-thin tissue paper, revealing a soft blush-pink fabric. Lillian looked up, then smiled at the worry on Liam's face. "Oh, Liam, it's magnificent!"

"How do you know? You haven't even looked at it yet."

He was right. Lillian slid the garment, a silk-and-lace nightgown, from the folds of tissue with an audible intake of breath.

"Why don't you go try it on, Elle?" said Liam with a catch in his voice.

"Now?" Lillian squeaked.

"Yes, now! I bought it for this occasion—even though I wasn't sure it would ever happen."

Lillian couldn't answer. If she moved, would the illusion end?

When Liam got up and took her hand to lead her inside to change, she let him.

Looking in the mirror, Lillian did not recognize herself. She'd never owned a store-bought garment before, and certainly nothing like this!

Then Liam was at the door, his face and neck ablaze with heat. Uncomfortable with his gaze, Lillian looked around the room and saw a vase of roses on the night stand. Liam had thought of everything.

He moved to her side. When she went to cross her arms over her breasts, he pinned them behind her. "Never hide yourself from me, Elle. You are perfect. Absolutely perfect."

Wrong or right, that's just how Lillian felt about him.

. . .

It had hurt, but only a little bit. Less than Lillian thought it might. And the pleasure! No one had described how it would be to feel so much pent-up desire and then have it released by the one you loved.

Afterwards, Lillian felt like a woman, no longer the schoolgirl she'd been only moments before.

. . .

Lillian and Liam learned to be very creative in finding the time and location for their lovemaking. Liam was careful, too, always pulling out just before his release. Two months later, however, Lillian began to feel tired and nauseous and knew something was wrong. Hiding the sounds of her retching had become impossible until one morning she found herself at the kitchen table with her mother.

"Is there something you want to tell me, Lillian, or do I have to ask?" said Eloise.

The quiet spoke volumes.

"No need," sighed Eloise. "It's obvious you're with child." Eloise knew it was Liam's baby. Of course, she had no one to blame but herself, seeing as how she'd encouraged them to be together, to treat each other as equals since the day they'd met. She shook her head and heaved an even greater sigh.

"You know there's nothing good that'll come of this, Lillian."

Lillian's sobs burst forth.

Eloise's sighing was no match for the tears of the girl. Taking her in her arms and rocking her like a baby, she thought about what was to be done. Most families would agree that the situation couldn't get much worse. Lillian's baby would tell the tale clear as day—clear as the color of the baby's skin. Most people would be diplomatic enough to close their eyes to it. Things like this happened all the time on the plantations when owners and bosses found a female sharecropper or servant who took their fancy.

Eloise had always considered herself lucky, what with Mrs. Jameson too busy being the southern socialite to hover over her help around the house. It wasn't slavery, per se, but it sure as heck wasn't freedom, either. Though the Jamesons had treated her well, she was under no illusion that once they found out about the baby they would feel threatened. Likely as not they'd think that Eloise's family, like so many others in debt, would try to capitalize on the Jamesons' son's predicament.

The truth was that such a family would not risk what they had, and the future of their firstborn son readying for the presidency, in the name of his bastard child. Eloise had often heard their conversations about how nothing and nobody would get in William's way as they steered him toward the White House.

Eloise had to think, and quickly. Lillian's belly would soon be showing, and there wasn't a soul on Jameson Plantation who would miss what was in front of their eyes, not with her daughter and William Jameson forever making moon eyes at each other. She made her decision. As much as she hated to send Lillian away, that was her only choice. "Lillian, there ain't but one answer here. You'll have to go stay with Aunt Jean in Aiken until this baby is born."

"No, Mamma, no. I love Liam. I won't tell nobody. I promise."

"Now, you listen here, girl, and you listen good," Eloise scolded. "You don't have to tell nobody. Everybody knows you been with that Liam. You ain't foolin' nobody, chil', nobody."

Eloise had been known to put the fear of God in some of the most manly men, but Lillian had never before felt it directed at her.

The thought of losing Liam was making Lillian sicker than her morning sickness.

"Get your head out of the clouds, girl," Eloise said briskly. "What do you think? You think y'all gonna get married? That Liam gonna up and marry you—a nigger girl? Sure enough not! He can't marry you, no sir. Yo' best bet is to go to Jean's. The Jamesons find out what you and that Liam have done, I don't know what they'll do, likely to kick us all right off the land, maybe worse. Then none of us will have no place to go. You know how they are about that boy." She took Lillian's chin in her hand. "Face it, girl. It just ain't gone work. You got to go."

Eloise pulled Lillian to her and held her tight. Lillian would be a lot better of down south, far away from the Jamesons' eyes, where she could deliver her baby in relative peace.

. . .

In Aiken, Lillian was a new face. She still wasn't showing yet, so the big question was why she'd come to stay with her "aunt" all of a sudden. But as her belly grew larger and rounder, there wasn't much sense in asking questions.

Lillian became the talk of the town. The women and young girls her age steered clear of her entirely, as if pregnancy were catching. The men practically ran from her, as if someone might blame them for her condition.

Denver Jackson was different.

One day, as Lillian did her errands, Denver tipped his hat to her.

"Howdy, miss. Where you off to this fine day?"

"I'm going where I'm going," said Lillian. By now she'd learned that avoiding all contact was easier than pretending politeness. 'Sides, her very soul still longed for Liam.

"Pretty and sassy," said Denver, picking up his pace to keep up with the lovely woman with her nose in the air. "I guess you must be the one causing so much talk 'round town."

Lillian rolled her eyes and kept walking.

"Well, thanks for asking, my name's Denver. Denver Jackson."

Lillian gave way to the handsome man who wouldn't go away. "Well, I'm Lillian, but I guess you probably know that, since everybody is talking about me and all."

"Mebbe so," admitted Denver, "but now it's official. Know what I mean?"

"Then why are you talking to me?" Then Lillian blushed. "Oh. I get it. You think I'm easy."

Denver stopped walking and put out his hand. "Now, hold on there, young lady. Slow down a minute. I think no such thing and have no such intention. I thought you could use a friend, that's all. But if you don't want to be bothered, I'll turn right around and leave you alone."

Taken aback, Lillian thought about it. She could use a friend, and this man, Denver Jackson, sure seemed polite and upstanding. She decided she'd let him hang about, but feign aggravation, as a nice girl would. At least for a while.

That was how it started. Denver took his time wooing the beautiful Lillian. He was there every day when it was time for her to walk home from her cleaning job, even when her belly got so big it was clear that nothing else could possibly be afoot. But Denver didn't appear to mind. He'd fallen for Lillian the first time he'd seen her, and he wasn't the type to care about what other people thought. Child or no child, he was not about to let her get away.

Lillian's feelings for Denver grew right along with her belly. The fact that he accepted her and her unborn child made her love him more and more. Soon they were married and, not long after Goldie was born, she found herself pregnant with Rose. The life they built together was perfect. She no longer thought about Liam, least not often, the white boy she'd left behind.

And that's why when the door shut behind him as he left for the sheriff's office she knew that life without Denver would be no life at all.

Chapter 6

Denver turned the corner on his way to the sheriff's, his mind churning with trepidation. He adored his wife and their girls and the life they had together. For a colored family in 1930's South Carolina, they didn't have it too bad, and he knew it. He had his own business and owned his home. He was still as in love with his wife as he was when he'd first met her, even if he had to share her with her friends. And his daughters would be the very first generation of Jacksons to go to college. He was not about to let anything change their plans.

No, siree. He would not let the likes of Cora Bidenfield take away all their hard-earned rights.

He opened the door to Bull Baker's office. "Mornin', Sheriff."

"Denver. I s'pose I know why you're here."

"I reckon you do, Sheriff. May I have a minute of your time?"

Denver had never begged for anything in his life on his own behalf. Was it about to come to that? The thought made him ill.

But he would do what he had to do for Lillian and the girls.

The sheriff waved him into a chair.

"Well, Denver, the news ain't so good, I'm afraid. Last I heard Cora hasn't changed her story. I did send John to talk to her and put his foot down—if you know what I mean," he added, appearing ill at ease for having made his own feelings clear at the injustice.

"I appreciate that, sir," said Denver, unwilling to spell out what they both knew.

"But, Denver, answer me this question. Why in the hell did Cora pick you out of all the boys in town?"

Now it was Denver's turn to squirm. "Well, Sheriff, I...."

"Go ahead, Denver. You can talk straight with me," said Bull.

Denver sighed and shifted in his seat. "Truth is, Sheriff, Cora Bidenfield's been after me since we were kids. But you know along with everyone else in Aiken that I love my wife. Always have." The sheriff nodded. "'Sides, even if I wasn't in love with Lillian, there's nothing in the world could get me to touch Mrs. Bidenfield. I've tried best I could and as respectably as I could to tell her no thank you. Somehow my, um, lack of interest, has only seemed to, um, make her feel all the more...um...amorous toward me."

The sheriff looked at Denver appraisingly.

"Well, I have to be honest, here, Denver. I don't know how this one is gonna play out. The only thing we can hope is that John Bidenfield can convince his wife to give up the name of the nigger she really was fooling around with."

The word rang out in the office. Bull's neck became red as an apple. Denver stayed quiet. He'd lived among whites his whole life and knew the ropes.

The sheriff continued, stammering a bit, abashed. "I...I can tell you one thing, though, that woman sho got it in for your ass."

The half-hearted joke fell flat, and the attempt at lightness disappeared like a wisp of smoke.

"I just hate the embarrassment this is causing Lillian. And you know as well as I do that Cora ain't much of a looker anyway."

"Careful now, Denver. You ain't supposed to be lookin'," Bull warned.

Denver didn't apologize, but Bull let it go.

"All right. This is what I believe is gone happen. Cora's not likely to change her story. Too much at stake. Me and the boys are goin' to have to pay you a visit. I'll inform them what's really goin' on first, instruct 'em to take it easy on you, rough you up a little bit. You know. Send a message to the other boys who might be so inclined to carry on with a white woman."

"But—but—" Denver sputtered. "That ain't fair, Sheriff!"

"Hell of a lot better than gettin' strung up from a tree, though, ain't it?" said Bull, already frustrated. "'Cause you know they're going to want some blood when word gets out what Cora's saying. Even if she is—between us, you understand—something of a, well, you know…. But unless you can come up with somebody else to take yo' place, that's the best I can do."

Denver sat back, disspirited. He was licked. He'd have to take his punishment, undeserved as it was, and thank the sheriff's white ass.

"Yessir, Sheriff," he said quietly. "I appreciate all you doin' for me."

"But Denver…for God's sake, listen to me. Don't fight back. The sooner we get this all over with, the better off it will be for everyone."

"Yeah, everyone 'cept us and the Jackson name."

Denver was up and gone before Bull could respond.

. . .

Sheriff Baker leaned back in his swivel chair and gazed at the photo of President Jameson on his wall. If times were different, he and Denver might be friends. But the best he could do was get to his buddies before word got out what Cora was saying. If they heard that Cora had been "raped" by a colored man there would be no way he could step in and stop the rage that would follow. Bull shuddered. It was time to get a message to his deputy, tell him to inform the others before the gossip got out of hand. Tonight was their regular meeting time at their place in the woods at the end of Whiskey Road, which served his purpose just right.

. . .

Deputy Billy Joe Brown resented being used as an errand boy. It surely was not in his job description. And neither was saving niggers. His job was locking them up.

When the sheriff gave him his orders that morning it was all he could do to keep from stepping over the line and insisting the sheriff be removed from his position for harboring fugitives. Instead, he'd docilely done what he was told, but hated that he hadn't spoken up. Denver Jackson lived in Bull's pocket, that much was clear. After "overhearing" the whole dang conversation between the two, Billy Joe even considered telling the others the wrong time. If they got tired enough waiting, they'd likely head out on their own, take justice in their own hands where it belonged. Without the sheriff there to keep the lid on things, there'd be no stopping the wheels of justice.

But Bull was the reason Deputy Brown had a job and home for his family. With his eighth-grade education, he wasn't likely to get a better one, neither. Especially not one that allowed him to wield so much power. So Deputy Brown swallowed his words and personally delivered a note to each man requesting they do their "civic duty" as ordered.

. . .

After he'd sent Deputy Brown on his way, Sheriff Baker went to the mayor's office. It was the sheriff's job to keep the mayor appraised of everything happening in Aiken. Mayor Zachary Stanton's office was located on Park Avenue in downtown, on the south side of the street, which was actually on the north side of Aiken because it was situated just past one of the bridges that connected the north to the south—white—side of town.

Aiken City Hall was a federalist-style building, rectangular in structure, with a large porch and cathedral-like entranceway. With its Gothic arches, tracery, and white Georgia marble in the entrance and balustrade and beautiful, robust ferns adorning every corner, no one was immune to its effect.

"Hey, Adeline, is the mayor busy?"

"Have a seat, Bull, I'll go check," instructed Adeline Roland, an attractive woman in her late thirties who probably wielded as much power as the mayor himself. Considered ahead of her time, what with having a full-time job while her children were in school, she also exercised regularly, something back then few people ever even thought about. On sunny days, Adeline could be seen with a big umbrella, instead of the usual hat of most women, over her head to protect herself from the harsh rays of the sun as she walked back and forth to work.

Adeline returned in a moment and gestured Bull through into the mayor's inner sanctum.

"Evenin', Mayor."

"Bull. How are you doin'?"

"Good, good. 'N' you, Sheriff?"

"Fine, fine."

Bull shut the door and sat down.

"I take it this is going to take a while," the mayor said drily.

Bull forced a chuckle and gave a half smile as he sat down in a chair clearly not built for a man of his size. The whole office was done up Victorian style, much too frou-frou for the sheriff's taste. All that fancy New York influence, he figured. But as long as Mayor Stanton took care of Bull, he could do his ol' office however he saw fit.

"I guess you all have heard about the mess Cora done got herself in, then?"

"I've heard some talk," admitted the mayor, "and I must say I'm not pleased with the nature of that talk. Furthermore, I hear the coloreds are planning a big meeting over on—"

"It's not like they can do anything," said Bull, knowing he was butting in.

The mayor did not like to be interrupted. "Hell yes, they can," he said, his voice rising. "See, there goes that small-mindedness of yours again, Sheriff. Coloreds with such things on their mind can cause a lot of fuss and bring the kind of attention we do not need to our fair city. The state of South Carolina needs to present itself to the country as a model state—one that has all its coloreds in check." He lowered his voice dangerously. "Don't you forget, Bull. We both have a lot at stake with the upcoming election."

Bull flushed, but kept his mouth shut. "Yes, sir, Mayor. I guess I lost sight there for a second."

"Then it's a good thing you have me to remind you, isn't it?" Mayor Stanton needled with a crafty smile. "I also heard you and your boys are planning to handle this situation as you always do."

Bull shifted uncomfortably in his lumpy chair and nodded.

"And just exactly how are you planning to go about it—or do I have to ask?"

"Now, just a second there, Mayor. I expect they'll be willing to wait until the real nigger who, um, was, um, with Mrs. Bidenfield is caught for the real work, but I probably can't talk the fellas out of making a bit of an example of Denver Jackson in the meantime."

"Tell me this, then, Sheriff. How do you think the coloreds are going to react when one of their most respected leaders has the shit kicked out of him?"

Again, Bull held back a retort. The mayor knew nothing about keeping the peace. All he knew was how to make speeches about his "fair city."

"It's the best we can do under the circumstances," the sheriff said, inserting a finger in his collar to loosen it from his neck to get a little air. "Look, they just goin' to rough him up a bit. That's all. I already spoke to Denver, tol' him not to fight back. He agreed that the sooner we get this over with, the better."

"Hmm. Well, then, it seems you've got everything under control there, Sheriff. You and your boys go ahead and teach those coloreds a little lesson with Denver Jackson. But when this other colored is found and slapped with a rape charge, you will arrest him and provide him with a fair trial the way any other civilized city in this country would do."

"With all due respect, Mayor," Bull said slowly, "this ain't any other city in the country. And it sho' ain't like the one you left up north. This is how we settle matters of this nature down here."

"With all due respect, Sheriff," retorted the mayor, "let me rephrase that for you. Perhaps I used some northern syntax that you didn't understand. If you want to handle security for the Blue Landing Club or any of the state functions I plan to hold in Aiken, you will conduct yourself like any other upstanding law official. If you don't, you may very well find yourself cleaning the same jail you used to run."

"There ain't no need for threats, now, Mayor," Bull protested, feeling the sweat pooling in his armpits. He was not happy with the turn of the conversation. This uppity northerner knew nothing about how things were handled in South Carolina or any other southern state.

The mayor sat forward and clasped his hands together on his desk.

"Bull, I promise you one thing. This is not a threat. Aiken must conduct itself like the elegant city that people believe it to be. We cannot have the Order running rampant, snatching up folk, and settling matters by taking the law into their hands, putting a stain on the culture, refinement, and elegance of our city. Don't forget, attendance was at an all-time high at this year's Triple Crown."

When Bull went to speak, the mayor held up his hand. "Now, now, I have no problem if you want to suit up from time to time and scare those folks with your robes and such. Nor can we have the coloreds rabble-rousing. So...."

Bull had had enough. "Damn uppity northerners!" he mumbled just loud enough for the mayor to hear.

The mayor looked at Bull hard. "And just who do you think fill the hotels, especially the crown jewel of Aiken, the Wilbridge Inn? Those same uppity northerners who come to vacation and end up building mansions. And who do you think benefits from the property taxes and the sales taxes we collect?" Mayor Stanton's eyebrows were high in his head, waiting for an answer.

"We all do," Bull grumbled reluctantly, seething inside.

"That's right, Sheriff," said the mayor as if Bull were his prize student. "Precisely. So if I let you and your boys go around killing folk, colored or not, we all lose. Honestly, I hate to see you running with that crowd, but this is not the time to quit them now. We need you to keep tabs on them. Speaking of which, what about that darn Jake Freeman? His reputation is rivaling that of Whiskey Road for trouble. Why haven't your boys got a hold of him yet?"

"You mean legal-like?" Bull was skeptical. The WWO would not readily want to tangle with Jake and his men, because for every man of the Order, Jake had three ready to die for him. "Mayor, if

I let my boys or the feds bring Jake in, he'd rat out other legitimate rum businesses faster 'n you can say alcohol." Bull delicately steered clear of calling them "rumrunners," since the mayor himself was one such man.

The illegality of alcohol in these Prohibition days didn't keep the Blue Landing Club, Mayor Stanton's side operation, for example, from continuing to serve it up. And Stanton was not about to give up running liquor. Not with all the luxury it afforded a family who was supposed to live on a mayor's salary. Though Stanton came from money, he was determined to build his fortune on his own, but do it in a way that came easiest.

In fact, in his mid-twenties, Zachary Stanton was the youngest mayor in the country, with the lofty "secret" goal of becoming the youngest president in United States history. His political career had started in high school, continued in college, and was showing no signs of slowing down.

The Blue Landing Club was another matter entirely. When Zachary Stanton Sr. died, Zachary Jr. inherited the club, which had come into the family through his mother. As it was not proper for a southern lady to run a business, even if she were originally a northerner, Emily Stanton had gladly fled the repressive south as soon as the earth had covered her husband's coffin. Even in death, however, Zachary Stanton Sr.'s strong-arm tactics were incentive for Zach Jr. to pursue a career in politics instead of the career on Wall Street that his father had chosen for him. The Blue Landing Club was simply another way to display his defiance.

Club members loved their sherry, champagne, and cognac, too. From all over the country they came, the roster including governors, senators, influential businessmen, and even a former president who'd vacationed in Aiken while in office. What with Zachary Stanton's connections, his election to mayor had been a shoe-in.

The mayor chose not to answer Bull's question. "As I was saying, I'll allow you this one time to teach the coloreds what they need to know, but you better make sure nothing regrettable happens to Denver Jackson. And you let me know what happens, Bull, soon as it's done. Not that I won't hear about it either way."

Bull left the mayor's office a lot more anxious than when he'd gotten there. What if things didn't go as planned? He needed to find out what the word was about town, and fast. There was one place he was sure to find out.

. . .

Bill Clemson's store was where people went to hear gossip, or more likely, to spread it. Clem's was perfect because just about everyone who went there was connected to someone else in Aiken. Located in the middle of town, just across the York Street Bridge, Clem's was frequented by whites, but was also the place where all the housekeepers chose to do their shopping, get updates from the local rumor mill, and bring it back to the north side. Cora Bidenfield's alleged rape would be front-page news by now, and every dark-skinned person in town would be on the lookout for signs of the WWO or an angry mob looking for revenge.

Clem was sitting on the porch chatting with four or five of his minions when Bull drove up. They went silent as he got out of his car. Talking about Cora's accusations, no doubt, Bull assumed, and about what they'd like to do with the perpetrator, Denver Jackson.

"Afternoon," Bull said, scanning their facial expressions.

"Bull." When Clem nodded, the others nodded, too. The usual camaraderie was nowhere to be found.

"Now, fellas, don't get all tight-lipped on me just 'cause I'm wearing a badge," Bull said. "I'm just another good ol' boy, like the rest of you."

"Yeah, and I'm the mayor," retorted Clem, letting go of a wad of chewing tobacco over the side of the railing.

The men burst out in loud guffaws.

"Okay, fine, that's the way y'all want it," said Bull. "But you know you're just dying to ask me about this here situation."

"Well, since you brought it up," Clem said snidely, "we might have heard a bit about this…situation, as you call it. And what we figure is that someone should pay."

Bull nodded sagely. "I couldn't agree more," he said.

The men looked up, surprised.

"You do?" asked Clem.

"Sure. The thing is…well…."

"Well what?" Clem demanded, moving forward as if to stand.

"Well," said Bull, taking his sweet time, "the things is that Cora, well, you all know how she is…."

"How she is?" parroted Clem. "How she is? Now what in tarnation do you mean by that?"

"Nothing really," said Bull smoothly, lowering his voice for effect. "Just that we all know about Cora's, um, appetite for the opposite sex."

There were smirks all around from the men, that is until Clem glared at them hard and they looked back down, chagrined.

"You telling us you don't believe that poor woman, raped like that in her own home?"

"Oh, no, no, nothing like that, Clem," said Bull. "It's just that the man she accused—you know, Denver Jackson?—well, he's the one man in this town wouldn't touch that woman with a ten-foot pole."

"And how you figure that, Sheriff Baker? Oh, yeah, yessiree, I almost forgot. Mister Denver Jackson is a friend of yours."

Bull had seen that one coming a mile away. "Now, Clem, you know there is no way in hell Denver Jackson or any of his kind is a friend of mine. He just happens to be one of 'em who causes me the least amount of trouble."

Clem spit a big wad of tobacco again, but missed the railing and it fell to the floor of the porch. The men all sat and looked at the brown mound on the floorboards as if it would up and walk away.

"Anyway," Clem said, "you're in luck, Sheriff. Me and the boys here? We're happy to look into this matter just to help you out. No use using all your resources over one scraggly-ass nigger."

Bull rolled his eyes. "Yeah, 'specially being that Cora is such a fine, upstanding woman and all."

"She still white!" hurled Bo Nathans from the sidelines.

"You're sure right about that, Bo," affirmed Bull. "And I thank you, Clem, for your offer of help. But me and the boys? We have everything we need to make sure justice will be served. We sure don't need any and everybody buttin' in makin' things worse." He looked at each man in turn. "And we certainly don't need no issues with the other side of town, if you know what I mean."

"Ain't nobody scared of them niggers," sneered Clem. "Let 'em get all riled up. We can deal with 'em."

"Yeah, I got some'um' for 'em," proclaimed Josh Whatley, a hot-headed plant worker who spent his time moaning about how his job at the facility was threatened by the black workers.

In reality, it was Josh's fellow whites that were the problem because the factory's management was renting black prisoners to work for a lot less pay. The management made a whole lot more profit and the states that rented out the prisoners made out like bandits, too. The practice had started in factories, but now blacks were being farmed out for profit to work in mines and on the railroads as well, and for almost nothing. Slave labor, same as usual. And now women and children along with them were working in various camps and brick yards. All it took was one misspoken word of "disrespect" to a white man (or woman) and the accusations came hurtling down.

"She stole my silver" or "He ran off with the pie." Didn't matter, as long as the accuser was white and the "perpetrator" was black.

Bull expected to see saliva drooling from their mouths, the men were so excited about the possibility of a clash where blood and savagery would be assured.

"Calm your heels, now, Josh," said Bull with just enough sternness in his voice. "Me and the boys got everything under control, and we will not stand for anybody—" he paused for effect "—for anybody to butt in. Are you all hearing me?"

There was silence while the men considered their options.

"Well now, Sheriff," Clem finally said. "Sure is nice to see y'all're on top of thangs round here."

Bull nodded. The bullshit was flying, but there was nothing he could do about it right now. He tipped his brim and turned to go.

He wasn't even full into his car when the cackling—and his own juggling act—began.

Chapter 7

Only about fifteen men showed up at the late 10 p.m. meeting. The others didn't want to get their hands dirty. They held onto their membership—you never knew when you might need the services of the Order—but lily white is as lily white does, and they had their image to think about.

Bull entered the meeting reluctantly, knowing that he was the one who had to convince this group that Denver Jackson, a colored man, was an innocent man and that Cora Bidenfield was nothing but a liar. He shouldn't have to convince them of something they already knew. They all knew Cora's reputation. They were simply looking for an excuse, and any would do, to carry out their own form of hate.

Bull's focus was on Charlie Stevens, the group's supreme leader. Whatever Charlie said to do, the rest would do it. But would Charlie believe that although Denver was innocent he'd be willing to take a beating for the sake of peace—that is, until that time when Cora revealed the truth? Under most circumstances a black person accused of raping a white woman would be hung. A hanging would get blacks all agitated, demanding justice for sure, and bring unwanted attention to the city while Mayor Stanton was so busy attracting bigwigs. Bull rocked on his heels as he waited for the meeting to begin.

James Newman, greens keeper at one of the local golf clubs, looked Bull's way and geared up to speak. "You can save your breath, Bull. We done already heard about Cora."

James Newman was a wannabe who wanted to be the leader of the Order. Badly. And all that money around him night and day led him to think he should have the same kind of money the club members had just 'cause he was around it so much.

"And what was it you heard…exactly?" said Bull. The amount of damage control Bull would have to do to save Denver's hide depended on how much buzz had already been disseminated.

"Yo' boy raped Cora Bidenfield," sneered Newman. "That's what we all heard."

"Now, see here, fellas, before y'all get too worked up, you should know the whole story."

"Let me guess. He didn't do it." John Myers' sarcasm cut through the air.

"Actually John, that's right. He didn't do it."

The brothers laughed, as if the whole thing were a joke.

"Well, Miss Cora Bidenfield seems to think he did, and that's good enough for us."

"Besides, you think we gone take the word of a nigger over Miss Cora?" It was Johnathon Appleton's turn to speak with righteous indignation.

"Johnathon, we all know what kind of a woman Miss Cora is," said Bull, placating as best he could. "I mean no disrespect to our fine white sister, but you know and I know that this ain't the first time she has put herself in a position…in this kind of a position… one where, let's just speculate here, in which she could say she'd

64

been attacked." Would avoiding the word "rape" idea, diffuse the circumstances even slightly?

Apparently not.

"Brothas, I think maybe we need to string up ol' Sheriff Baker here for disrespecting our white women with such a suggestion," Andrew Little chimed in. Little owned a mechanics garage and ran a juke joint out of it at night. He and Bull had been archenemies from the get-go and then, when Prohibition swung into effect and Bull made him pay a small fee to sell liquor, the stakes had gone up. Little felt that as a brother in hate he deserved a break.

"Shut the hell up, Andy," barked Bull impatiently. "All I'm saying is we have all heard the rumors about Cora's appetite for dark meat. Now, I certainly hope you ain't putting her in the same category as our wives, mothers, and daughters."

This declaration was met with silence.

"Still, she deserves the same protection as any other white woman," Appleton said.

"Listen here," said Bull. "I happen to know for a fact that Cora is using Denver Jackson as a cover for her affair with another colored man. And I know you all don't want to let the real culprit get away with messing with a white woman."

"I say we get them both, then," returned Little, the most bloodthirsty of them all.

"But she's not saying who the real one is," Bull said, rolling his eyes. "Y'all gonna let your thirst for blood condemn an innocent man and let a guilty nigger go free?"

"Well, what the hell do you propose we do, then, Bull?"

Bobby Chisholm wasn't quite willing yet to have the blood of an innocent man on his hands. A farmer and deacon in the church he attended as well as the chaplain for Aiken's chapter of the World of the White Order, he often justified the supremacy of the white race by quoting the Bible and opened each meeting with Leviticus 25:44-46: "They shall be your possession. And ye shall take them as an inheritance for your children after you, to inherit them as a possession; they shall be your bondmen forever."

"This just shows that they can't think for themselves and make moral decisions," Bobby went on self-righteously. "They need us to keep them under control."

"Bobby's right, Bull. We can't let this charge go unanswered," James Newman agreed.

"That's right. Them niggers'll think it's okay to take our women anytime they feel like it, and we can't have that shit," snarled Andrew Little.

Bull held up his hand. "All right. All right. That's enough. Here's what I'm thinkin'. We need to send a message. We show up at Denver Jackson's and whip on his ass to teach them all a lesson." At this, a glint formed in the eye of every man there, but Bull kept going.

"Keep in mind, we are only sending a warning. Nothing more. After that, we just wait. When Cora believes everything has died down, she'll continue to see whoever it is she's trying to protect. All we got to do is stake out her place and catch him. That's when we can give due justice."

"Bullshit. I say we get 'em both! Andrew Little spat. "Send a real message to those boys."

Again Bull held up his hand. "Now, hold yo' horses, y'all. Don't forget Denver Jackson is a leader to them. They know he didn't do it. Hell, even I know he didn't do it. Taking him out will set them off, and we can't afford that kind of aggravation."

"Bull...shee-it," whooped Andrew. He pointed at the sheriff. "Our good sheriff here is just trying to keep things quiet for the mayor so as he won't get those clean hands dirty."

Bull shouldn't have been surprised, but he was. Unfortunately, if these men had put two and two together, so would others.

"That's right. Stanton can't run for no senate if he can't control those savages here in Aiken, can he?"

Bull didn't have time to formulate a response before Johnathon Appleton put in his two cents. "Maybe you'd better calm down here, Andrew. Bull might be right."

Andrew glowered, but stayed silent. Appleton was known for his levelheadedness and held a certain clout.

"The niggers generally stay on their side of town; we stay on ours. Other than Cora we got 'em trained pretty damn good." Appleton looked over at Charlie, who hadn't said anything for a while. "Charlie, you sittin' there kinda quiet. What you got to say 'bout the matta?"

Bull prayed Charlie would side with him.

Charlie took his sweet time answering. "Well, for once, I'd say Bull makes sense. Taking out two of 'em in close proximity might bring the feds down here to snoop around. We don't need that. I say we send one heck of a message through Denver Jackson, like Bull here says, and wait on Cora to hang her nigger when the time comes."

Bull felt his shoulders fall back down into place slightly.

"Well then, it's settled," said John Myers. He owned the other lawn business in Aiken, the one that competed with Jackson for the white business. Nearly half of Aiken preferred to do business with Myers rather than pay a colored man who was in competition with a white man.

But Andrew Little wasn't finished. "Hold on, there, John. What in the hell you mean, it's settled? You of all people should want justice carried out to the fullest extent. Denver Jackson been cuttin' into your bu'iness for years. It ain't right that a nigger make near about as much money as one of our own."

Of course they all knew this was a bald-faced lie. The whites who used Denver Jackson's service paid less than half of Myers' prices.

"Calm down, Andrew. I couldn't take on Jackson's business even if I wanted to—and for the record, I don't. At my age, I don't want to have to hire folk and deal with all those aggravations, neither. So getting rid of Jackson won't do me any favors."

Andrew Little harrumphed, but sat back.

Silence fell.

Bull stepped in before anyone else could. "All righty, then. We're agreed. We'll pay Denver Jackson a little courtesy visit while we wait for Cora to hang herself—or whoever her visitor was, I should say."

There were reluctant nods all around, Little's last, but there nonetheless.

Bull felt his relief through his whole body, which had been tense as a metal pole since the meeting had begun. Denver Jackson was a good man, and yes, a friend of his—at least as much as any white man could be friends with a colored man. Jackson couldn't help it that he was born that way.

Chapter 8

Denver dreaded telling his wife about his conversation with the sheriff. She'd want to pack up and leave Aiken even more than she had before. He'd just have to make her see this so-called solution Bull had cooked up was the lesser of two evils. Bull knew Denver wasn't their man, least he had that on his side. And he'd had beatings before. Not that he'd look forward to it, but still…. There didn't seem to be any good alternative. All the way home he thought about how to break the news to his precious wife.

"Lillian? I'm home."

One look at the kitchen and Denver knew all he needed to know. When Lillian was anxious, she cleaned to settle her nerves. He'd never seen the kitchen so spotless.

Denver walked over and gave his wife a kiss on the forehead.

Lillian put aside the sponge in her hand. Only one other man had ever kissed her on the forehead like that. Given the current circumstances, the realization was jarring. She took a deep breath. "Tell me, Denver. What did the sheriff say?"

"I'm not gone beat around the bush, darling. The way it stands now, if Cora don't tell the truth, I'll be the one to answer for it."

Denver braced for the fallout, then reached out when Lillian swayed on her feet. She brushed his arm aside, angry, and sat down at the table.

"You?" Lillian whispered. "What does that mean? The sheriff is going to condone killing someone they know is innocent on account of that no-account whore?"

Denver looked at her, shocked, but she wasn't done.

"Oh, what am I talking about anyway? There's no justice down here for us. Never has been and never will be!"

Lillian's expression of fear and anger was horrible for Denver to see. He again put out his arms to console her. Again she pushed him away.

Denver stepped back. "Now see here, Lillian. Get a hold of yourself. We have to think this through."

"Think it through? There's nothing to think through anymore. We have to leave. We can't stay here. They'll kill you."

"Baby, you know I can't cut and run."

"'Cut and run?' There's no shame in leaving. We can start over in Virginia with my people there."

"Lillian, you know I'm not going to live off your family. Besides, I'm innocent. How is it gone to look if I run from this situation with Cora? They'll hunt me down like a dog. No. I've made up my mind. Ever' last one of them are going to have to look this innocent man in the eye."

"And do it for the last time, maybe! If we go, you'll still be alive, Denver. But, it you don't want to go to Virginia, that's all right. We can go up north...to Canada, maybe."

Denver shook his head.

Lillian deflated. "At least let me write the President, then."

"Who? Did you say the President of the United States? What, you done gone plum crazy, woman?"

"Denver, listen to me. I haven't lost my mind." Lillian pulled out a chair. "Sit down. There is something I need to tell you."

Denver reluctantly sat. "I guess you gone tell me that you know the President personally or some such nonsense."

Lillian looked him in the eye. "Denver, you know I love you, right?" Denver nodded suspiciously. Where was she going with all this fool talk about the President?

"And you know that I have loved you since I first came to Aiken with my unborn child and you showed me kindness, patience, and acceptance."

Denver waved his arm impatiently. "Git to the darn point, woman!"

"I'll git there soon enough," said Lillian. "Just hold your horses."

Lillian sighed. She had hoped never to have this conversation, yet here they were.

"You know I came from a wealthy plantation, right?" Denver nodded. "Well, what you don't know is that it was one of the wealthiest plantations in the whole country. My family had stayed on to sharecrop. Mamma worked in the kitchen. She practically ran the house. I stayed with her, had the full run of the place with the owners' boy, who was just about my age. His mamma had little use for him, so he spent most of his time with us."

Denver had gone very still. Lillian felt she might faint. But she'd started and could not very well stop now.

"Liam—that was his name, Liam—loved Mamma like his own. Anyway, Liam and I were best friends. He taught me to read, Denver—read!—and gave me every book he had when he was done reading it. He taught me French, too."

Denver looked up sharply. Suddenly, he knew exactly where this was going. His body went stone cold.

Lillian saw the comprehension on his face. "Yes, Denver. Yes. I...we...we fell in love. I...I got pregnant. That's why I had to leave. Mamma was afraid the family would be sent away."

"That doesn't make sense, Lillian," said Denver in a cold voice Lillian had never heard before. "Things like that happen all the time. Kids like that are a dime a dozen, treated like any other child, regardless of the father. Why would yours be any different?"

"Because our child"—Denver winced—"would be the child of the man being groomed for the presidency."

Denver jumped up so fast he knocked over the jelly jar of flowers on the table. Lillian reached for it, but it was too late. The water pooled and then dripped over the edge.

Lillian spoke quietly. "My family was in a lot of debt to the Jamesons, Denver. Mamma was sure they would assume that with such information they would be ripe for blackmail. After all, who wouldn't want to use what we had to get out of debt?

"You're right that one more baby 'tween a colored girl and a white boy was nothin' new. Heck, white boys are raised to take girls whenever it suits them. But in this case, this boy was supposed to be president, and the Jamesons wouldn't let anything or anyone get in their way, let alone some colored baby.

"I had to go, Denver." She looked up at his face, pale and disturbed. "And you know the rest."

. . .

It took a few minutes for Denver to collect himself.

"You mean to tell me that our little Goldie's daddy is President of the United States? President William Jameson?"

Lillian nodded. "That's exactly what I'm telling you."

"And you want me to ask that man to help me? Now I know you done lost your damn mind."

Tears sprung to Lillian's eyes. Never, in all the years they had known each other, had Denver cursed at her directly. Immediately, Denver regretted his words. He sat back down and took Lillian's hands in his own.

"I cannot do what you're asking me to do, Lillian. I can't. But Bull gave me his word. He has assured me that if I don't fight back"—now it was Lillian's turn to wince—"that it'll all be over soon enough. Eventually Cora will come clean and the whole thing will blow over. At least for us."

"You can't really believe that, Denver! You really trust that sheriff so much?"

"Bull might be a good ol' boy, Lillian, but I've known him to be a man of his word. He hasn't lied to me yet."

"But the others, Denver! How can one man speak for all those others?"

PART 2

Chapter 9

"You're telling me that my granddaddy, Granddaddy Denver, was willing to take his chances on the word of a white sheriff with ties to a hate group? And that your father was President William Jameson? I don't even know what to say."

Goldie opened her mouth to speak, but Shelby wasn't near finished. "How come you never told me this before? Who else knows?"

Goldie clucked. So many questions. But, to be fair, Shelby had a right to know her history.

"One question at a time, darlin', one question at a time. First, your granddaddy and the sheriff had developed a mutual respect for each other. Bull's word had always been good in the past, and Denver was certain it would be this time as well."

"But—" inserted Shelby in a huff.

"No 'buts' about it, Shelby. Denver Jackson expected he could trust the sheriff as he had before. And remember, times were different then. He did what he thought was best."

Shelby nodded, but her eyes glistened with tears.

"And, to be honest, talking about my 'real' daddy would be nothing more than a lie. Denver Jackson was my real father from the moment he stepped into my mother's life."

Shelby nodded again, her head down.

Rose took Goldie's hand. "Poor Mamma and Daddy. They were caught no matter which way they turned. They wouldn't tell us what was going on, just sent us to our rooms to do homework. Mamma made sandwiches, tol' us to eat in our rooms and stay there for the rest of the night. That had never, ever happened before. That's how we knew something real bad was coming, right Goldie?"

Goldie bit her lip. "We sure enough did, Rose. And I'll never forget waking up in the middle of the night to Mamma's screams."

"We all watched at the window. The white men came to the porch and called for Daddy to come out. Then they lit into him."

"But why did he go outside like that? Why did he leave the house?" asked Shelby, tears staining her cheeks.

Rose's voice trembled. "'Cause if he didn't, they would have come in and got him. And that was not something he would want any of us to see."

"Was it the WWO?"

The sisters nodded. "Sure was," said Rose. "About fifteen of them in all. They formed a circle around Daddy, taunted him, tried to make him angry so he'd fight. He stood fast, though. Refused to react. They said all manner of nasty, vile things about all of us, Mamma, Goldie, and me. Seems Daddy truly believed they'd stop on their own. It did no good, of course. When they saw their words weren't doing the trick, they gave up trying to rile him and went to it anyway. Punched Daddy to the ground, kicked him good, passing him around the circle so they could all have their fill."

"When they saw Daddy was unconscious they backed off and stood there, just looking at him on the ground," said Goldie.

"But I thought—"

"No, Shelby," said Goldie. "I know what you thought, but Daddy wasn't dead. Not yet, anyway. Mamma wanted to run out and minister to him, but we held her back. She was crying and screaming. Those men outside didn't care one whit."

"Then Daddy came to," said Rose.

"That's right," said Goldie. "And it was as if he were possessed. He rushed at the men, left, then right, raging at them with his fists, his head, his legs.

"Course, it was one man against an army. And these were some of the most bloodthirsty men in the county. Andrew Little? He was having the time of his life. One look in his eyes and you knew he wouldn't leave until our daddy was dead."

Rose continued. "Then, somehow, Daddy got a hold of Timothy Green. We don't really know what happened, it was over so fast. But suddenly Timothy Green was lying on the ground— dead—and the men let out a yell fit for the devil. A minute later, they dragged Daddy off into one of their trucks. If they couldn't kill him for raping Cora Bidenfield, they surely could for 'murdering' one of their own. For that was surely what they'd call it.

"It was the last we saw of him. Alive, that is."

Stunned, Shelby looked from her mother to her aunt.

They nodded in unison.

"Turns out they took him into the woods and hung him from a tree. Uncle Ronny found him swinging there the next morning."

"But what about the sheriff?" demanded Shelby. "What kind of a man—"

"The sheriff?" said Goldie. "Well, you know how it is. The man didn't have a chance against so many with a different code. He apologized to Mamma with his hat in his hand. Not that it helped any, of course. It sure couldn't bring Daddy back to us."

"The White Order knew they had the wrong man, but someone had to pay," said Rose, shaking her head. "Cavorting with a white woman was a crime punishable by death. This time that someone was Denver Jackson."

. . .

"Mamma just wasn't the same after that," said Rose. Goldie nodded her agreement. "She ran the house, took care of us girls, but couldn't seem to move on from the love she had for Daddy. Not until she and Pitney reconnected, that is."

Shelby's eyebrows had been rising higher and higher. At this point, they practically reached her hairline. "You mean...?"

"Yes," said Goldie. "That I do. Mamma's 'friendship' with Pitney raised many a brow back then. She and Pitney were ahead of their time, it's true, but nobody really knew how deep their friendship went.

"They didn't try to hide it, either. They'd been friends since Denver had intervened with the sheriff to get Pitney's husband out of jail for public drunkenness way back when."

"What happened to Pitney's husband?" asked Shelby.

"Leland? That mean ol' sonovabitch? He didn't dare lay his hands on her—she'd have none of that—but he sure did withhold affection. Went weeks and weeks without touching her, not even on the hand. Acted like he couldn't bear to look at her."

"That's so sad," said Shelby.

The sisters agreed.

"Pitney was lonely, even with her children for company. Lillian's friendship was just what she needed."

Rose nodded again sagely. Feeling loved was as important as breathing air.

"It's a lot to take in," Shelby said quietly. "Are you saying Grandma Lillian...was a lesbian?"

"Well, we didn't use that name for it back then, of course, not that anyone really knew, not even us. But you know how people are, make something up if they don't know the facts."

The three nodded together.

"Mamma's so-called friends believed the worst, naturally, and if the others hadn't taken Daddy's business away from her, they would have found a way to do it."

"They took the business away?" Shelby asked, aghast.

Rose gave a mirthless chuckle. "Listen up, my dear. I'm about to school you about how things worked in the Bible Belt. You listening?"

Shelby rearranged herself on the bed, not wanting to miss a word.

"John Myers—you remember him?—well, he owned that competing lawn business in Aiken. Daddy got whatever business Mr. Myers didn't get or want, but that didn't mean Daddy wasn't successful. On the contrary. So, after poor Daddy's demise, it seems Mr. Myers had a change of heart. Seems all that business that looked much too taxing afore his death was no longer quite so taxing. But there was one problem. Mamma."

Goldie bit her lip as she recalled the scene Rose described.

"To circumvent having to deal with the likes of our Mamma, Mr. John Myers convinced the Green family to petition the court for 'compensation for wrongful death of the head of household.' The courts did as bid, naturally, just as quick as that, and snatched Daddy's business as restitution for Timothy Green's 'unnatural' death. Since Mrs. Green did not want the business, she sold it lickety-split to Myers and put the money aside for a dowry for her next husband."

"Um-hm," agreed Goldie. "Lickety split."

Rose continued. "Aiken Greens is still there, though, you know, the oldest lawn company in the state of South Carolina. You can take pride, Shelby, knowing that half that business belonged to your family."

"We got jobs to help Mamma out," said Rose. "And we were determined to go to college. Daddy was adamant we go to school in Orangeburg. I guess it's called South Carolina State University now. Then, it was one of the few colleges in the state where blacks were allowed. Mamma and Daddy wanted us to be teachers. I guess we wanted it, too." She grinned at Goldie. "But sometimes things have a way of changing the best of plans, don't they, Goldie?"

Chapter 10

Jake Freeman was his own man, and he let everyone know it.

Perhaps that was what initially drew Goldie to him. Or perhaps it was his self-assured swagger. Either way, by the time they caught each other's eye, the die was cast.

Jake's reputation preceded him, of course, for his willingness (which some might call it pigheadedness) to take on the Order. But after the World of the White Order had taken Goldie's beloved daddy, her family's security, and her innocence, Jake appeared to Goldie as more of a hero than anything else. She despised the WWO with all her heart, but the fact was that she despised having to go work for white people a thousand times more. She wasn't cut out for cleaning! She and Rose had been raised to set their sights on college, not kitchens. Yet they had to swallow their pride every single day to help support the family.

When Jake first laid eyes on Goldie, something had snapped inside him, as if he were a new violin string being plucked for the very first time. He'd known her as a child, but this was a new Goldie, one who apparently had grown up overnight before his eyes.

He pined to see the light brown hair with its natural caramel highlights that she kept pinned up cascading down her back. He pictured her in beautiful dresses that he'd buy for her, though even her work clothes of the plainest cloth enticed him to come closer. Nothing would stand in his way, he decided. Not his business; not her family. Jake caught up with her one day on her usual route to work and slipped into stride next to her.

"It's Goldie, right?"

Goldie slid her eyes in his direction, but kept walking forward at a fast clip. She knew who he was, but wouldn't admit to it.

"You have me at a disadvantage, sir, since I do not know you at all."

"Well then, let me introduce myself," said Jake, removing his hat with a flourish. "Jake. Jake Freeman, at your service."

Goldie was so tongue-tied she stayed silent, by far the least incriminating approach.

Jake put his hat over his heart. "I sure hope your silence does not mean you've been given the wrong impression about me?"

"Im...impression?" stumbled Goldie. "What impression would that be?"

Jake smiled. "We both know how Aiken can be, now, don't we? Time things get retold and retold, the story's often very different from the truth."

Goldie knew she couldn't trust this man from here to the street lamp. But he was so handsome, and charming as well. It couldn't hurt to walk along with him for a while.

After another minute or two they'd reached the corner of the street where Goldie kept house for the Stantons. She skittered away from Jake's side, but he put his arm out to touch her elbow.

"Listen, Miss Goldie. I'd like to say...well, if you all ever need anything, anything at all, I'd like to think you could call on me to help."

They both knew that Mrs. Jackson would have none of the likes of Jake Freeman, but Goldie nodded politely before turning back to the house and disappearing through the screen door, which slapped behind her. She made it just in time, too. Mayor Stanton's wife did not look kindly on tardiness.

. . .

Jake thought about his meeting with the luscious Goldie Jackson on and off all day as he went about his business affairs. Her chocolate-brown eyes swam before him like pools of deep water. And that smooth skin! Why, she was fresh as a daisy!

He immediately went to work to supply protection for the Jackson family. A couple of men around the house two or three nights a week was a good start, and one she would not have to know about. In the meantime, he solidified his plan to be in the vicinity whenever Goldie was accessible.

Goldie, meantime, chastised herself severely. First, for allowing Jake Freeman to keep her company like that; second because she'd liked it so much. And then, third, because she knew if Mamma ever heard that she was keeping Jake Freeman's company, she'd never hear the end of it. Sighing her way through her work that day, she reminded herself over and over that Jake was a bad boy, and not right for her.

It didn't dissuade her one little bit. She was hooked.

. . .

Jake's criminal status was unavoidable. But even those law-abiding churchgoers who looked askance at his activities were willing to overlook those same activities because Jake was unafraid to thumb his nose at the whites. Especially since he was in direct competition with the exclusive Blue Landing Club.

Stories abounded about Jake's business dealings, like the one about the night he ran into Sheriff Baker on Park Avenue, just after receiving his shipment of hooch and on his way back to his side of town.

"Evening, Jake," the sheriff had said, tipping his hat. (Least that's how the story went.)

"Sheriff." Jake thanked his lucky stars that he hadn't decided to take home a bottle with him that night.

"I believe you got something for me," said the sheriff.

Jake sighed. He'd been paying off the sheriff for years and was plum tired of their "agreement." The sheriff did nothing but hide behind his badge. Just look what'd happened to poor ol' Denver Jackson.

"Now, Jake, let's not dance this little jig again. It's been a long day and I'd like to get home for my dinner. Just hand over your payment and I'll be on my way."

Jake glared at Bull. The sheriff glared back.

"Don't you know by now you can't win, Jake? In this battle you are sure to come up short."

"Oh, you see it that way, do you?" Jake snorted.

"I surely do," said the sheriff. "You know as well as I do that any difficulties between us will only mean trouble for the rest of yo' people."

Jake seethed with contempt. "Why, you sonova...." he started, but stopped at the look on the sheriff's face. He began again. "Hiding behind that mask and hurting innocent people is bad enough. But you are the same man 'my people' are supposed to be able to call on to protect them from your brothers. The same ones who are only too happy to string them up from any tree with a branch."

The sheriff set down his hat on the still-ticking hood of his car. "You prepared to do something about that, Jake?"

Jake stepped into the street. He never was one to back away from a fight and this time he was ready and willing.

Bull was forced to reconsider. Was he being foolhardy to rush into a tussle? Public relations being what they were right now, it was best to keep his cool. "Just hold up, there, Jake. Lucky for you, your ass will avoid the whooping I intend for it, at least for tonight. But once the elections are over—well, we will have some unfinished business to attend to."

Jake stepped back onto the sidewalk and grinned. "I'll be counting the days, sheriff, counting the days."

Bull held out his palm. "Now, like I said, give me my damn money and I'll be on my way."

Jake reached into his pocket and pulled out a large stack of cash as Bull spoke over his shoulder.

"Fellas, we got ourselves one arrogant nigger here tonight. Any interest in setting him straight?"

Why, that sonovabitch! thought Jake.

The bills safely in Bull's hand, he stepped aside as ten men with rifles, pipes, and knives moved in to surround Jake right there on Park Avenue. Other than Jake, the sheriff, and the men, it was as if everyone else had moved away. The street was empty, as if they knew to stay in their houses and lock them up tight.

John Myers spoke first. "Let's take him down right now and put him out of his misery. That way he and his strays won't lust after our wives, mothers, and sisters."

Jake's upper lip curled up in disgust. "Please. You think we interested in yo' women? Women like the fancy Miss Cora Bidenfield? No one wants a piece o' that no more."

"Whoo-ee, just look at this nigger, y'all," said John Appleton. "Thinks just 'cause he runs a juke joint he's more than what God made him, a lowly speck on the road." He spat at Jake's shoes and moved in.

Suddenly two figures emerged from the shadows. "Fellas," said Jake. "Nice to see ya."

"Jake."

The men, big, muscular, and carrying clubs, were poised for a battle.

Andrew Little made a sound something like a garbled gasp, though later he would swear on the Bible he had only cursed as he readied for the fight.

. . .

Apparently, it was over before it ever really got to going.

Soon other figures had come out of the shadows, from behind the trees and bushes, to stand behind Jake. All totaled, there were eighteen of them before they stopped coming.

It seems the sight of them took away the voices of the men in the street, who stood rocking on their heels spitting fire but unable to light the match. They were clearly outnumbered.

Finally, the sheriff had spoken into the night. "All right, all right, no need of this getting out of hand. We don't need no blood bath in the streets of Aiken. Why don't you boys just get on home?"

When no one moved, Bull spoke again, louder this time, "Get on home, now, y' hear? We'll settle this matter another time."

Slowly the men surrounding Jake backed up, but did not take their eyes from the faces of the black men in front of them.

"Go on," said the sheriff. "Jake, you, too. Time to git back to your side of town. And take yo' men with you."

Jake gave the sheriff one very long look before he, too, faded back into the shadows.

Chapter 11

"Jake Freeman was fierce!" Shelby said, clapping her hands together. "Tell me more! I want to hear all the stories!"

"Now, now, Shelby," said Goldie. "Can't tell such things all at once. But you're right about one thing. Jake Freeman was one fine individual."

"Um-hm," said Rose. "That man might have been the handsomest man around—white or black—if not for the likes of our daddy—and my beloved John from Spartanburg, of course."

"Hush, Rose! That's no way to talk," said Goldie, waving at her sister.

"It's true and you know it," said Rose. "Your daddy, Shelby, was lusted after by just about every woman in the state. But he didn't let it go to his head. He was loyal as they come. Though I must admit, he did have a quick temper, didn't he, Goldie?"

"He did that," said Goldie. "Had a few altercations in his day, too. Rumors were that he killed a man somewhere along the line, but no one was ever brave enough to ask, least not in our family."

The sisters nodded some more.

"He was from a good family of his own, though, Jake was," Rose went on. "Owned a farm and a general store. A beautiful home on the north side of town. Jake, he was the youngest of five. They all went off to college, but Jake had an adventurous streak in him that could not be satisfied sitting in a classroom. He was likely the smartest of the bunch, but not one for school learning."

"Jake started working for Nate Williams when he was just fifteen years old," said Goldie. "His father was very displeased because Nate Williams ran a nightclub and some other ventures on the side. But Nate took to Jake like a son. As a teenager he started out by running errands for Nate."

"Errands?" Shelby squinted at her mother. "What kind of errands?"

"Well, I'm sure I don't know," said Goldie, looking the picture of innocence. "There were suggestions that it might be something illegal, of course, but we never believed a word of it. Did we, Rose?"

Rose pursed her lips and nodded. They both knew what Nate, and then Jake, had been up to, but it would never pass their lips.

"Jake worked his way up the ladder until he was Nate's right-hand man," Goldie said. "Then poor Nate had a heart attack. To everyone's surprise, he'd left everything to Jake, who was now the proprietor of the hottest nightspot in town, Nate's Place, and all at the ripe old age of nineteen."

Goldie got a glint in her eye. "Oh, those were some good days back then. Even some of the white folk went to Nate's Place when they were looking for a really good time. We knew not to let the sun go down on us on the south side, but they could do whatever they wanted on the north side." She sighed at yet one more injustice in the long list of injustices they had suffered.

"When Prohibition really came on strong, there was nothing Jake could do," said Rose. "To keep the club open he had to go from quasi-respectable business owner to all-out rumrunner. The money was just too good to give up."

"Well, he surely had no intention of returning to his farm!" said Goldie. "If that meant doing business with th   ... occasionally, then he did what he had to do.

"Naturally, a deal with Sheriff Baker was part and parcel of that deal. For a share of the profits—and a healthy share, too, I might add—Sheriff Baker agreed to look the other way regarding the shipments and selling of liquor." Goldie laughed. "Jake was even nervy enough to broker a deal with the WWO a time or two. In return, they agreed not to harass his patrons on the way home after a night of partying. As long as they got their cut they were generally appeased."

Rose shook her head. "Greed," she said. "Makes a follower of most men, I'm afraid."

Shelby nodded along. Nothing had changed in the world in that regard, she figured.

"But Jake had a soft side, too," said Rose, "one he kept special for Goldie. He begged her to marry him, of course, but his business would expose her to a lifestyle that he worried would put her in danger. He talked about going legit, about advocating for the reversal of Prohibition. He was tired of paying off Bull to satisfy the law and paying off the WWO to keep his patrons safe."

"For the whites, Jake was a big ol' thorn in their side, making so much money as he was, and powerful to boot. When he started selling hooch to joints in Georgia and North Carolina, they threatened to shut him down, but no one had the stomach for it, I guess," Goldie said. "Besides, he was ready with men who had the weapons and the heart to tangle with the Order any time, day or night—usually night, of course, because the men in the Order were too cowardly to carry out their wicked deeds in broad daylight."

Rose tsked. "Aiken was a small town during the Prohibition years, but it was big enough to be a major player when it came to liquor. Which led to the unfortunate increase in crime as well, and not just any crime, but organized crime. But not like the big cities. Somehow Aiken avoided the gangs, murder, and mayhem. We had what they call "victimless" crime—if you can believe that the crimes carried out by the WWO were victimless!"

Shelby heard the bitterness in Rose's voice. This was a part of history that made them all downright ill.

"But with all law enforcement on the take, well, you can imagine the circumstances."

Shelby nodded vigorously.

"And all those men, good ol' southern boys every single one, never missing a Sunday at church. Sheriff Baker right along with them. They called him a God-fearing man, but the only ones he feared were those above him on the totem pole of power. Fact is, only time the sheriff left Aiken was to escort Mayor Stanton to the Capitol."

Goldie nodded. "Bull's loyalty was pulled betwixt and between for a long time, but in the end he was a loyal member of the World of the White Order who cared more for money than men."

"But, Mamma, how do you know so much about these dealings between Daddy, Sheriff Baker, and the liquor marshals?"

"Don't you recall, Shelby? I worked for Zachary Stanton, started there after Daddy was murdered. You don't know how it was back then. Blacks were to be seen, not heard. We were often privy to private conversations, and truth be told, I made sure to place myself where I would be. We needed all the inside information we could get in those days to save our own skins."

"So we did," said Rose, "so we did. Remember that Ol' Miss? Oh, the secrets we heard that woman tell."

"Miss who?" asked Shelby, confused.

"That's what the slaves called the wives of the plantation owners, Shelby—Ol' Miss—just so they wouldn't know what we were talking about. This time we were speaking of Caroline Stanton herself. But that's a story for another day—or at least a few hours."

Shelby protested, but couldn't get another word out of her mother and aunt. Her curiosity would have to wait until they were rested. She shut off the light and tiptoed out of the room.

. . .

Prohibition was practically impossible to enforce. The fact that many liquor marshals lost their lives added to the very problems the law was supposed to correct. For every liquor ring that was busted, another "legitimate" business emerged. Grape juice could be easily turned into wine. "Near beer," containing a half percent alcohol and added to real beer, easily made it past the usual regulations. But the most abundant legal alcohol use was for medicinal purposes— "medicine" that contained ninety-five percent alcohol—and likely responsible for an increased number of alcohol-related deaths, drunkenness, and drunk driving. Such maneuvering soon had the ultra conservatives up in arms, which only led to the need for those involved in liquor consumption to find a way to dupe these groups as well as the feds.

Sheriff Baker and Mayor Zachary Stanton were only two of those plotting to ensure the well of liquor would never go dry.

Zachary Stanton was elected mayor shortly after Congress passed the Prohibition Act, and soon thereafter Aiken developed a reputation as the place where those who imbibed could get their fill. Mayor Stanton, however, found himself in something of a fix due to the double life he was living. On the one hand, he had his hand in the grand till of rum-running; on the other, he aspired to greatness in politics and dine with the ones with the power.

The line Mayor Stanton walked became narrower with every step. He needed Jake Freeman to provide the liquor for the Blue Landing Club where the demand was constant, but was required to act the part of a man of distinction when it came to supporting the law. He skirted the issue by appointing someone to handle the day-to-day operations, staying in the background where he hoped no one would look too closely at his activities. With his wife's extravagant tastes in all things blue blood, keeping the money rolling was top priority.

"It was Zach's wife who caused so much ruckus," said Goldie.

She and Rose had taken a nice long nap and were now in the kitchen with Shelby, big cups of tea, and thick slices of rum cake. "Um-um-um, this sure is good," she said, helping herself to another slice.

Shelby was impatient to hear more, but the storytellers would not be hurried. Finally, appetites assuaged, Goldie picked up the thread.

"She wasn't one to keep up with the Jones as much as desire to be one of them herself. Caroline was born and bred in New York and never let a soul forget it for a moment. And her dresses! My, oh my! Even her day wear looked like evening wear to most of us in Aiken. She wore flapper dresses like they were going out of style, placing her orders every day of the week."

"And her stockings were real silk," said Rose.

"Um-hm," agreed Goldie. "I washed many a pair in that house of hers and, let me tell you, the times I thought about putting runs in a pair or two...."

"Mamma!" said Shelby.

"Well, I did! But don't worry. I never did anything, though it sure was tempting. Not that a cook and laundry maid like myself needed to get myself accused of any wrongdoing."

Shelby looked stricken.

"Now, baby," said Goldie, patting her hand, "you gotta do what you gotta do. I did it in the hopes that one day you wouldn't have to. If that meant cleaning Caroline Stanton's drawers, then that's what I did."

"Amen to that." Rose's nose joined Goldie's pointed toward the ceiling, a pose that made Shelby smile.

"Now, back to Caroline," Goldie said. "She was no slouch, this woman. Although I do believe her family's money, ah, helped along the situation. Course, I'm just telling you how it appeared," she said. "But Aiken was small potatoes for her kind, even the grand Whiskey Road estate, neighbor to the Blue Landing Club, which her husband, now the mayor, owned.

"The house was mostly hidden from view from Whiskey Road by a high brick wall. All you could see from the street was the third story. Pink crepe myrtle trees and willow trees lined the long curving drive." Goldie's voice was dreamy in recollection. "The front lawn and porch were adorned with roses, azaleas, and various flowering shrubs. Right in the middle of the front lawn was a magnificent live oak tree almost as tall as the house, and around that big ol' oak tree draped with gray-green mantles of moss were five magnolia trees whose aroma guided you right up to the main house. That's where the Stantons liked to entertain family and friends on Sunday evenings for coffee and dessert. 'Course, when they really wanted to do it up, they'd send engraved invitations for black tie affairs in the ballroom."

"Didn't all the estates have names?" Shelby asked.

"They sure did," said Goldie. "This one was the Manhattan. That's what they called the antebellum-style home, one of only a few in Aiken. It had a gable roof that sloped down to the eaves on all four sides, making it appear symmetrical when you looked at it

.he outside, even with all its elaborate balconies and porches columns and such."

"Tell her the good stuff," huffed Rose, who'd never been particularly fond of architectural discussions.

Shelby waited. "The good stuff?"

"Now, don't pay her any mind," Goldie said, but smiled with a secret in her eyes.

"Mamma, come on, don't make me beg...."

"Okay, okay. Hold onto your hat, dear. It's just that Mr. Stanton, well, it seems he was just the slightest bit sweet on me, which meant he often forgot to hold his tongue when I was in the vicinity."

"He was what?"

"Well, the truth is the truth," said Goldie—a little snippily, Shelby thought.

"But how did you know?"

"Baby, if you don't know when a man is sweet on you, I didn't raise you right," Goldie said. They all chuckled. "I knew, that's all. The way a woman always knows. 'Sides, sometimes I got a little extra money on pay day or an extra day off—not that Miss Caroline was too pleased about it."

Shelby breathed in. "His wife knew he was sweet on you?"

Goldie shook her head. "Sweetie, a woman always knows when her man is sweet on someone else. And she didn't like it, complained about my work or about needing me on my day off...or just about anything that she felt like."

. . .

"I've had about enough of this, Zachary. There is absolutely nothing that girl has done to deserve a day off, and I need her here, helping me."

Zach thought quick before his wife could a make her mind up that there was more to this situation than met the eye.

"Come on, now, darlin'," he said, mooning at her with the bedroom eyes she'd loved so much when she agreed to marry him, "the poor girl—"

"Excuse me? What did I just hear you say? That 'poor girl'?"

Oops.

Caroline's foot had begun a harsh rata-tap-tap on the floor. "Just because her family had a little money before her father died, you think she deserves better? She's nothing but another colored who wants to rise above her station. We don't owe her a thing."

Zachary realized his blunder immediately. "You're right, of course, sugar, of course. I was simply thinking of you."

Caroline's foot stopped and she looked at her husband suspiciously. "Me? Really? In what way does giving that girl the day off benefit me?"

"Well," said Zach, angling for time, "I just thought that, well, with all the overseeing you have to do when the help is here and all...that you could use a break. You're always saying that having them around can be such a burden, allows you no privacy, isn't that right?"

Caroline's suspicion went down, but only a notch. "I suppose," she said grudgingly.

"Besides, one day Goldie might surprise us all and head off to that college she's always chattering on about."

"Zach! She'll be lucky if she makes head housekeeper one day, let alone finds her way to a college degree," poo-pooed Caroline. "Now, Mr. Soon-to-be-Senator, if you're done with all this nonsense, come help me into that new emerald dress you bought me before I get it in my head to make you sleep on the chaise tonight."

Zachary obliged without complaint, grateful for his ability to pull off yet another coup de grace.

. . .

As Caroline and Zachary were gussying up for their night out with the current senator and his wife at the Blue Landing Club, Laney Baker was fixing dinner for her family. She and Bull Baker had two boys, but the three ate like six. Seemed every time she turned around she was cooking another meal. In fact, Laney had grown so familiar with the entire process that she could daydream right through the process from setting out the ingredients to putting it on the table without burning a thing.

Today, Laney's fantasy was centered around Zach and Caroline Stanton, who had matching Fords—a Model A, for Zach, and the other a Model T for Caroline's very own. 'Course, Miss Caroline rarely drove, but merely owning such an automobile was cause for one's heart to thump in one's chest.

Laney Baker longed for the riches of Caroline Stanton, the community standing, the freedom. She longed for the day when her maid would be doing the cooking and she, Laney, could spend her time on much more important things. Like going to the club and sittin' around the pool with a mint julep in her hand.

She sighed. When Bull married her she'd been nothing but a down-home country girl. Problem was, he'd expected her to stay that way. Oh, she was grateful enough for their three-bedroom home, a far cry from the shack in which she'd been raised as the daughter of a sharecropper. Not that they were down there on the lowest rung of the ladder with the niggers, of course. It had simply been a matter of self-preservation. With three girls and no sons, every hand had been needed on the farm.

Besides, who needed more of an eighth-grade education to be a wife and mother? Her lessons had come in the form of practicing the social graces in order to fit in with the upper echelons of Aiken society. Just remembering the mayor's last Christmas party, to which she and Bull had been invited, gave her goose bumps.

Bull came up behind her. "Umm-um! It sho' smells good in here!"

"Just the way you like it," said Laney. She knew more about pleasing her man than just about any other woman in town could say about theirs.

Bull finished off his plate of fried chicken, mashed potatoes, and greens in a flash, then was off to work, smacking Laney on the bottom on his way out the door. She giggled, loving it all.

Except the fact that he was leaving again. Seemed like all he did nowadays was eat, smack her bottom, and go to work.

She called out to her boys to go do their chores and hoped her husband would return before it was too late for some hanky-panky.

. . .

Once again, the first stop on Bull's list was Clem's Country Store, where he'd get caught up on all the gossip. Clem, often his son Jeb, and the other locals could be found at the store more often than their homes. One of them was June Bug Lawson, a not-too-bright but hardworking man who didn't seem to be clued in to the fact that his son was suspiciously dark-skinned.

June Bug had married Lara Smith, his school sweetheart. Unfortunately, Lara's heart belonged to another, that of Justin Holmes, a young black man who helped his father deliver the Smith's meat to their general store. The Smiths weren't what you might call wealthy, but they owned property and hired help. Back then, such status was considered middle class. Lara, the eldest of three girls, was aware that she wasn't especially bright and would therefore have to marry well. There was only one thing that appeared to be getting in her way—her interest in colored boys, particularly the one named Justin Holmes. And the older she got, the more interested she became.

One day, after Justin's father had injured his back, Justin was scheduled to make a delivery of meat to the Smith home. Since all the Smiths were at the store for the summer clearance sale, one of them had to be sent home to accept the delivery. Lara volunteered.

Exactly nine months to the day, Lara gave birth to her first child. But in the eight months in between, she'd attached herself to June Bug Adams, the most trusting knucklehead she knew. Though June Bug may have questioned the timing of this birth, he chose not to upset the applecart, given his love for the lovely Lara. In all the ensuing years, no one ever said one word to June Bug, either, some assuming he knew the whole story and chose to ignore his wife's proclivities and some assuming he was just too dumb to figure it out.

"Mornin', June Bug. How's the family?"

June Bug waved at Bull and pulled his chair up closer to the railing, the better to hang his boots over the edge. Ed Hawkins was in the next chair, another average southern man. Ed worked at the stables with June Bug and also worked for John Myers in his landscaping business. The third man, Jesse Lee, ran a delivery business, rum being only one of the items on his roster. Eli, number four, didn't seem to do much other than hang out at the store. Including Clem, that made five. On that porch, the friends discussed politics and women and everything in between.

"Fine, fine," said June Bug.

"Say, Bull," Clem said. "Hear tell that Jackson girl is working for our good mayor."

Bull nodded. "Since what happened to her daddy."

There were a few snickers, but no one chose to bring up the death of the Jackson girl's father.

"For a nigger gal, that one ain't too hard on the eyes, know what I mean? I got a few jobs I could use her for myself." Clem guffawed at his own wit. The others followed suit.

Bull never was quite comfortable with this kind of talk, especially not as relating to Denver Jackson's daughter. And especially after what had happened.

"Real shame what happened to that girl's pappy," Eli weighed in.

Bull couldn't quite tell how much of this statement was couched in sarcasm, but if he had to guess it would be up there at about ninety-nine-point-nine percent.

"Shit. Just one less nigger we got to worry about getting at our women," said Ed.

"'Course Cora...now there's a woman knows how to take her pleasure," said Clem. "You had a piece o' that pie at some time, didn't ya, Bull?"

Clem was determined to stir the pot. But before Bull could respond, Ed chimed in. "Who hasn't?" he jeered.

Since everyone knew that Ed shared a small home with a distant cousin and the rumors continued to fly about their relationship, this insinuation fell on deaf ears. Homosexuality was illegal, of course, but the people of Aiken had chosen to let the question of Ed's sexuality slide, preferring ignorance over outrage.

Clem ignored the comment. "Sure was big of Stanton to help those Jackson girls find work, now wasn't it?" he said.

Bull declined to answer yet again, adjusting his hat with discomfort.

"If our good mayor isn't doing that girl, I'll eat my hat," Clem went on.

"All right, Clem, that's enough," Bull warned finally, not that he hadn't had the same thought himself, if he were being downright honest.

"Come on, now, Bull. You know them northerners like that dark meat."

"Northerners? Look around you, Clem. There's plenty of fair-skinned niggers walking 'round Aiken, if you get my drift."

Clem went still. In the resulting silence all you could hear were the cicadas and mosquitos.

Then he said, "Not that Zach Stanton would do anything to jeopardize his sterling reputation—or the club's reputation, neither."

Bull was reminded how Clem's membership application had been turned down at the Blue Landing. No wonder he had it out for the mayor.

"Clem, shut your trap, you hear me?" said Bull. "I'm already tired of the direction of this here conversation."

But Clem wasn't done. "I hear he's salivatin' at the chance to run for Senator Johnson's seat, too."

Bull galred at Clem but then shrugged, feigning lack of knowledge more than in-difference. There was no real news here. He'd best be on his way.

"Where you headed, then, Bull?" asked June Bug.

"The north side," he said shortly, and turned heel to go.

Chapter 12

"Don't tell me you were interested in that Zachary Stanton, Mamma!"

Goldie was affronted. "Shelby! 'Course I wasn't! But his interest in me made things difficult. That, plus my Mamma's opinion of Jake, of course. And now things were heating up on all the rumrunners."

"You weren't afraid to be involved with someone like...like that?"

"Never," said Goldie. "That man was nothing but kind and loving to me. And very protective. Right, Rosie?"

"That man worshipped the ground you walked on, sure enough, Goldie," Rose said. "Put those men to watch the house, too, thinking we wouldn't notice." She clucked. "Now, I ask you, who wouldn't be aware of something like that?"

"What did Grandmother have to say about it?" asked Shelby.

"She didn't particularly approve of Jake and his business, but we all felt safer for it, even your grandmother."

"But why would there be any reason to harm Grandmother or you girls? Grandpappa was dead!"

"Simple math equation, my dear," said Rose. "We were three women living alone. There was no one to keep any of them from returning in one of their Halloween costumes to do whatever damage they might think up."

Shelby sighed, feeling the truth in her aunt's words.

Rose went on. "Jake's men would have done anything he asked them to do. He had charisma! They were drawn to him like moths to a flame."

"Alas," said Goldie. "That's how the real trouble started. You see, as the sheriff busied himself making sure he was getting his share of the take to support his and his wife Laney's up-and-coming needs, he forgot to pay attention to the fact that the higher he placed his tariffs, the more customers decided to take their business to Jake, where they could get more for less.

"No—" said Goldie, anticipating Shelby's next question, "they didn't like buying from a black man, but economics'll win out every day of the week. Soon, club owners from all over Aiken County and Augusta were buying from Jake Freeman—not to mention all the locals."

"My, how the sheriff began to smart about that," said Rose.

"Um-hm," Goldie agreed. "And my boss—Mayor Stanton— did not appreciate the ramifications either. He complained about it to Miss Caroline all the time. Course he didn't share the fact that it was partly his ego that was suffering as well as his pocketbook. He knew it was again time to discuss things with the sheriff. Personally."

. . .

It was already late when Bull knocked on the Stantons' door, annoyed at the summons. He was tired of being ordered about at the whim of this man, the "future" whatever it was. Where was the benefit for Bull? Where was his plush estate? Where were his

104

fancy parties? For that matter, why wasn't he asked to sit in on the important meetings the mayor conducted with other officials? Shouldn't he be included as a trusted law man?

The door was opened by none other than His Majesty. The help must have been retired for the evening. It was that late.

"Evenin', Sheriff Baker."

"Mayor."

"Thanks for coming."

As if he had a choice.

They went into the mayor's study. "Drink?"

Bull declined after a slight pause. It wouldn't do for the mayor to gather any ammunition on Bull, which meant the sheriff would not let down his guard. Stanton had no idea that the very man he wanted Bull to take down was the same one who was paying the sheriff to look the other way.

Goldie Jackson appeared a moment later, asking if there were anything the mayor needed before she left for the night. Aha, thought Bull. One member of the help who hadn't been dismissed along with the others. Interesting.

The mayor, about to pour his own drink, had Goldie do it for him. The naked lust on Zach Stanton's face made Bull burn with anger and shame.

While they waited for Goldie to finish, the mayor began his discourse. "Well, Sheriff, it seems things are moving right along."

Bull nodded, choosing to remain mute and keeping Goldie in his periphery.

"I have a few things lined up, but I will need your help to make sure the city is on its best behavior."

"Whatever you say, Mayor."

There was an awkward silence.

"Something wrong, Bull? If there is, you'd better fess up now, 'fore we take another step farther."

105

Bull glared at the mayor who, he decided, had the sense of a mule. "No, ain't nuthin' wrong." He looked pointedly at Goldie.

"Oh," chuckled Stanton. "You remember Goldie Jackson, don't you, Bull? My most trusted employee."

Already? Bull wanted to ask. The girl hadn't been working there more 'n a few weeks. But again he stayed quiet, nodding politely at Goldie, who went about her business, although a slight flush had crept up her face. When she was done and had handed the mayor his sherry, she waited.

"That's all, Goldie. You're free to go," said the mayor, and turned his back.

Goldie's expression did not change as she pivoted and left the room.

"I'll get straight to the point, Bull. We have to do something about these damn rum-runners. The situation is getting out of hand."

Outside the room, Goldie carefully left the door ajar a bit so she could listen to any plotting that might take place between the mayor and the sheriff. She knew the subject was rum-running, and that meant the subject was also Jake Freeman. She cupped her ear to the door, held her breath, and listened, praying that Miss Caroline would not take it into her head to stray downstairs.

"I've got senators, congressmen, and businessmen scheduled to be present during my announcement speech next week. I will not relish the moment appropriately if rumors are flying around about Jake Freeman. Nor do I want to risk any strife between Freeman's gang and yours." Stanton's stress on yours put Bull on notice once again that the mayor experienced displeasure at the WWO's proclivity for violence.

"Stanton," said Bull with a growl. "I ain't so stupid that I don't know when I'm being insulted. If that's what you dragged me over here for, then I'll just—"

The mayor waved him aside like a gnat. "Come down off that high horse, Bull. You know I'm right." Bull went to argue the point, but the mayor put up his hand. "Either way, I didn't call you here to discuss the moral justifications of your friends. You know where I stand on that issue, so we'll move right along."

Depends on what day it is, thought Bull.

"Now, I've got Senator Jantzen from New York." He handed Bull a pad and pen from his desk. "You may want to take this down."

Bull rolled his eyes, but took the pad and pen.

"Then there's Moseley from New Hampshire...and Senator Montreaux from Louisiana. They'll all be staying at the Wilbridge Inn for the weekend, and I do not want them being bothered by locals, so post a deputy there 'round the clock. All we need is some coloreds getting the idea to run their mouths about how you all do things down here in the south."

Bull stabbed at the note pad, seething at Stanton's condescension. Here the man professed to dislike their "methods" in the south regarding race issues, but wouldn't do a thing about it if it would jeopardize his shot at the Senate.

The mayor went on. "Congressman Byrnes of District Three and Congressman Lane of District Two will be here to represent the National Federal Party's endorsement of my campaign. Congressman Mayweather from Georgia will be in attendance as well. They'll be staying at the Blue Landing Club, so you'll need another deputy there as well. The mayors of Columbia and Augusta will attend, but do not plan to spend the night."

"Do you need a deputy to watch over them as well?" Bull didn't bother to hide his sarcasm, but the mayor either didn't catch it or chose to look past the infraction.

"No," said Stanton, "that won't be necessary. Reporters will also be here from various newspapers, and I don't mean Aiken and Augusta, but from all over the country. We cannot afford any negative coverage from coloreds who decide to make some kind of statement."

The mayor lowered his voice. "Now, listen carefully, Bull. This here's the sensitive part. I rely on you to make sure it does not go beyond these four walls."

Outside the door, Goldie wished the mayor would speak up. Her legs and neck were stiff from standing utterly still to avoid creaking the floor boards, but she stayed put, sensing whatever came next would be important.

"To ensure the coloreds stay home and tend to their affairs, it might be necessary for a few of your men to ride through the north side of town. Not in full regalia, mind you. Just a couple of cars making the rounds, keeping an eye on things, letting their presence be known. You know what I mean."

Bull couldn't believe his ears. "Let me see if I'm getting this straight, Mayor. You are asking for help from the very same men you claim are so immoral?"

"I believe it's best to look at it a little differently," said the mayor loftily. "Think of it like this, Sheriff. This gives your friends the chance to do something good for a change. Why, keeping the peace'll benefit everyone in Aiken."

"Northerners." Bull shook his head.

"Excuse me?"

"You think you are so morally superior because you appear to do more than tolerate the coloreds. When, in fact, you don't really tolerate them at all. You just got them thinkin' you do, and they too ignorant to know it."

"Touché, mon frère," said Stanton and saluted the sheriff with his glass.

"Too what?"

The mayor sighed. "Never mind. But all that is irrelevant to our situation. Treatment of coloreds may not be much better up north, but toleration swings on a pendulum, and right now it is heading north along with your field workers. You think about that when you don't have anyone to pick your cotton, clean your houses, or work in your factories. And think about how this will be a record year for South Carolina in collecting rent for its prisoners."

Satisfied he had won the round, Stanton ended there. Bull was not in his league, and sparring with someone so clearly uneducated and uncultured was beneath someone of his position.

"And one other thing before you go," he said. "The National Federal Party has asked the President of the United States to introduce me as a senatorial candidate."

"No, shit. I'll get to meet President Jameson?" asked Bull, wide-eyed, momentarily forgetting his disgust.

Stanton glared at him. "No. What I mean is, you better keep your fellas as well as the coloreds in check so this thing goes off without a hitch."

At the look on Bull's face, Stanton threw the poor sheriff a bone. "I tell you what, Sheriff. If things go perfectly smoothly, I'll see if I can squeeze in a handshake for you and your lovely wife."

Bull nodded, thinking about how thrilled Laney would be to impress her friends by shaking hands with the President. He put on his hat and started to rise.

"Uh, Bull, there is one more thing. I need you to get Freeman to close his place for the weekend. We cannot have drunkards roaming the streets late at night. And NO deliveries—other than mine, which as you know is arriving on Tuesday."

"Um, I don't think I'm gone be able to get him to close shop completely," Bull said. Stanton had no idea that Freeman got his liquor from the same runner as the Blue Landing Club.

"What do you mean, you can't? You're the goddamn sheriff, for crying out loud."

Bull back-stepped. "I mean to say, we shouldn't. Not unless you want to piss off the locals. They're likely to take to the streets if I shut their place down. And knowing bigwigs are in town will only be an incentive to cause a scene. They'll have Freeman's men right behind 'em, too, and they ain't packin' light, if you know what I mean."

The mayor considered. "Well, that's a damn shame. You mean to tell me between the mayor and the sheriff we can't shut down a colored club? What can we do?"

It was Bull's turn to consider. "Well, I can meet with Freeman, ask him to hold back on availability so as not to encourage—"

"Un-fucking-believable," said Stanton, banging his glass down on the desk. "You're going to meet with Jake Freeman and ask for a favor?"

"Now listen here, Stanton," Bull snapped. "If you so much smarter than me, how come you don't know Freeman gets his hooch from the same runner as you? For all you know, he prolly got records on every time your club gets a stash. I guess you might think about messing with him twice 'fore you cause one o' your 'scenes.'"

Just outside the door Goldie gasped, then clasped her hand over her mouth, again praying to the Lord that the men were too engaged to hear anything.

Damn, that felt good, thought Bull. He'd just stuck a big pin in Mayor Stanton's bubble.

Stanton turned red as a ripe watermelon. "What!"

"You heard me. You get your hooch from the same runner as Freeman."

"And you've been keeping this from me?"

"What the hell difference would it make? You goin' to stop serving your sherry, your fine wines, and old-ass liquors? I don't think so. 'Sides, everything is under control. Everyone is getting what they want."

The mayor went still. "I'm disappointed in you, Sheriff. This makes me look like I'm no better than Jake Freeman. How could you do this to me?"

"I didn't do nothin' to you," the sheriff blustered.

"I beg to differ," said Stanton coldly. "I count on you to keep me apprised of everything going on in this town." He shook his head as if his disappointment in Bull were the saddest thing he'd ever experienced. "But we'll have to set this matter aside for another time. In the meantime, put together a plan about how to execute the plan we laid out tonight, you hear?"

He led Bull to the door.

Just before Stanton closed the door, Bull remembered his wife's request. "Oh, Mayor, my wife Laney says to tell Caroline she'll be calling on her to get together sometime."

It was the mayor's turn to seethe. "I sure will, Sheriff, I sure will."

Chapter 13

Although Goldie would be even later than usual getting home, she needed to make a detour. The roar of the band Nate hired to perform Thursday through Saturday nights could be heard clear across the street as she rounded the corner.

Being Jake Freeman's woman came with privileges that Goldie had grown to appreciate. She had always received attention for her looks, but now she got respect along with it. As she strolled through the bar, the revelers parted the way as she headed for Jake's office.

Jake was sitting at his desk.

"Goldie! What are you doing here?"

"It's not a bad time, is it, Jake?"

"'Course not," said Jake, standing up to greet Goldie properly with a few moments of intimacy. "You just now getting off work?"

"Yes, but—"

"Why are you still working out there, anyway? You know I would prefer you quit altogether."

"Jake, you know I have to help out at home, and don't even start! Mamma won't accept one penny from you. Besides, when I tell you what I heard tonight, I think you'll reconsider."

Jake pulled Goldie to the settee and they sat down. "Tell me everything."

"Well, Sheriff Baker came by to see Mayor Stanton just as I was about to leave for the night."

Jake looked at her expectantly.

"Well, unfortunately, I had to hide outside the door, so I didn't hear as—"

"You did what?" yelped Jake. "You could have gotten killed for less, Goldie! What were you thinking?"

"Now don't go getting all in a huff," Goldie said. "When you hear what I heard, you'll appreciate the need for me to stay."

"This had better be good," said Jake sullenly.

"Course, I couldn't hear all the words," Goldie admitted, "but first they talked about their plans for the weekend of the mayor's speech, about how the sheriff needs to keep the city in check, put on a good law-abiding face for all the muckety-mucks coming into town—including the President of the United States!"

Jake pursed his lips. "The President! Huh..."

"But wait. There's more," said Goldie. "They had an argument before the sheriff left. And I'm pretty sure it was about you."

Jake picked up Goldie's small hand in his own bigger, stronger one. "Goldie, you know I've never liked to lie. But sometimes we have to do things that don't conform to the current legalities. I'm promising you...that is, I'm sure that if we can hold on a little while longer, we will be back on the right side of that fence."

"But Jake, that's not what—it's just that—"

"Now, I don't want you to worry your pretty little head about what I do for a living or what the sheriff and the mayor were spouting. I can take care of myself."

"I know, but—"

"No buts, Goldie. Listen to me. I deal with the same people that Mayor Stanton knows."

"Still. They must be planning something big. Sheriff Baker stayed late and he wasn't happy when he left."

Jake held her hard. "You're certain he didn't see you, Goldie?!"

Goldie hastened to reassure Jake that he had not.

"Then we are done with this discussion." Jake held her chin in his warm hand. "I appreciate your looking out for me, but I do not want you putting yourself in danger. Am I clear?"

"Clear," said Goldie grudgingly. "One hundred percent."

. . .

Goldie practically ran home to avoid her mother's wrath. Jake didn't hold out much hope around the President's intentions. He always said politicians made lots of promises they couldn't—or wouldn't—keep. Goldie herself felt that President Jameson might be different, though. She knew a number of her people who would have voted for him and were talking about supporting him the next time around, as well as other National Federal Party candidates. Switching from the State Party, the party that gave them their freedom, was not an easy decision, but Former President DeJanes had driven the country, and especially the African Americans, into the ground with his "pull yourself up by the bootstraps" philosophy.

Besides, President Jameson was talking about programs to help the poor and disabled. He wanted to improve public works in the south. It was exciting to imagine everyone having electricity, running water, and telephones. And the President's wife talked a lot about women's rights. That alone was worth switching parties for, as far as Goldie was concerned. What was the point of having laws like the Nineteenth Amendment giving women the right to vote and the Fifteenth Amendment saying a citizen can't be denied the right to vote based on that citizen's "race, color, or previous condition of servitude" if no one was benefitting from them? Then there were all those poll taxes and property requirements. Goldie was the first to admit it was a bleak picture. But that's why she held such high hopes for this president.

By the time Goldie reached home, she was no longer thinking about politics, however. Instead, it was the passionate kiss of her lover that captured her senses.

. . .

"Hey, Mamma."

"You're late, Goldie. That man keep you again to take on some fool chore?"

"Nothing like that," Goldie hedged. "They're all in a tizzy over there because of all the goings-on next weekend."

"Goings-on?"

"You know. All the politicians coming into town. Miss Stanton is all up in arms about what she'll be wearing at all the events and the mayor is meeting with...with everyone under the sun."

Her mother harrumphed. "To discuss how to handle us, I'll bet."

Goldie wisely kept her mouth closed. "Where's Rose? Is she asleep already?"

"I think she's still up waiting on you."

"Well, goodnight, then, Mamma. I'm off to bed."

Goldie leaned in to give her mother a goodnight kiss. She might be in love with the biggest rumrunner in the south, but she'd never be too old to kiss her mother goodnight.

Chapter 14

The next morning, the Jacksons rose early to prepare for church. They had their usual Sunday breakfast of grits and fish with a side of eggs. Lillian always looked forward to church, but today more than usual because they were holding a meeting to discuss several important community issues, and the widow of Denver Jackson was not one to just sit there looking pretty and nodding agreement with the men when there was work to be done.

Denver had always encouraged Lillian to speak her mind, and it had become second nature to her. She was fully aware that it was only her status as his widow that offered her that latitude with the other members in the beginning. Once they recognized that Lillian could be counted on for an endless supply of good ideas and good common sense, however, even the more difficult, more reserved men began to come around.

Truthfully, Lillian hadn't grieved long. Openly, that is. She'd put her efforts directly into the causes where she felt she could do the most good. As a member of the new national civil rights group, for example, she was part of the movement to push Congress to outlaw lynching. Their petition had been denied, of course, but Lillian would not be deterred. In fact, she had prepared some notes to share with the congregation today. On their way to church, she rehearsed what she was going to say.

As they approached the steps of the sanctuary, Lillian turned an appraising eye at her daughters to confirm they were squared away and presentable. After smoothing down Goldie's skirt and brushing a few crumbs off Rose's blouse with a tsk-tsk, the three went through the double doors. Church was the one place where you were expected to shine in your most presentable regalia. They took their usual seats in the fifth pew by the aisle.

The choir had already begun singing today's opening hymn, "Wade in the Water." To many ears, this was simply one of the many hymns sung in many black churches, but today, in this church, it was a signal that important matters were to be deliberated and all were invited to attend. With the words "God's gone trouble the water," all could infer that certain factions were about to stir the pot.

After the opening song, the church secretary, Mrs. Teresa Williams, made her announcements and then led the church into meet and fellowship. Accordingly, the congregants turned to their neighbors and said their good mornings and how-do-you-dos. After that, Deacon Fryer led the Lord's Prayer and then came the responsive reading, Psalms 36:5-6, 40:10, and 89:1-2.

Lillian found the choice of these verses interesting, given they talked about faithfulness—and not just to the Lord. The verses had the added message of reminding the congregation of their responsibility to the cause. After the reading, the church was led in a soft hymn. As the ushers in white gloves collected the tithes and offerings, an offertory prayer of blessing was said; immediately thereafter, those who wished could go up to the altar to receive a special prayer.

Lillian was grateful for the small fan she had brought as the warmth of the church filled with so many bodies began to cause her to feel drowsy. She was also grateful that the preacher, who tended to be long-winded on a good day, would likely reign himself in due to the upcoming meeting.

Lillian wanted to set a good example for her daughters, but had a tough time sitting still that day. When the preacher finally concluded his sermon, she let out a long sigh of relief, which caused both her girls to grin. Nobody knew better than they that their mother was far more interested in what would happen after church than during the service. "So," said the preacher, "if anyone has to get home, you may exit now. Have a blessed week. Look out for one another as you would yourself."

Though uncomfortably hot now, there were not many who left the church, only the few elderly with their escorts.

It was time to get down to business.

. . .

"As you all know," Pastor Bell stated once people had resettled themselves, "Aiken is expecting some heavy hitters next weekend. We are gathered today to discuss how to take advantage of the situation to further our cause, and are blessed to have a special guest with us to do that. Mr. Winthrop Pennington is from the National Civil Rights Organization. The NCRO has just started a chapter in Columbia and is looking to start one in Aiken." There was murmuring in the congregation. Pastor Bell held up his hands. "I will now turn over the floor to Mr. Pennington."

As Pastor Bell spoke, a white man who'd been sitting in the back stood up. There was a stir among the parishioners and a number of the ladies adjourned to the back of the church. Not Lillian and her girls. They intended to be right up front where the action was, no matter what form it came in. The white man walked down to the front of the room, appearing not the least bit ill at ease at being in an all-black church in the south.

"Good afternoon, church," Mr. Pennington opened.

"Good afternoon," responded the congregation, staring wide-eyed at the newcomer as if he had three heads.

"My name is Winthrop Pennington and, as Pastor Bell stated, I am with the National Civil Rights Organization. I am here because you—no, we—have a unique opportunity to make a statement next weekend in your city. With the arrival of the sitting president and the dignitaries he'll bring with him, we can cause the world to sit up and take notice about the oppression you are still suffering throughout the south."

There were nods and "amens" all around and people shuffled in their sticky seats.

Mr. Pennington continued. "What I propose is that we hold a march. Go all out with signs and bullhorns. I am prepared to call for reinforcements from my colleagues at the organization. A hundred demonstrators could be down here to march with us next weekend. All you need to do is give me the say-so."

"Here we go," said a voice from the pew parallel to the Jacksons'. Mr. Brown was known for his vocal commentary, and obviously would not disappoint in this meeting. "No disrespect, Mr. Pennington, but you white, and you sure look like just another northerner come down here to stir up trouble in our community. When you—and your 'colleagues'—leave, that's what we'll have, too. Lots and lots of trouble.

"You think these damn—" Mr. Brown gazed at the ceiling "—'scuse me Lord—hate groups care two cents for your civil rights?"

"And you are...?" Mr. Pennington asked calmly.

"Brown's my name."

"Well then, Mr. Brown, I assure you we are prepared to stay after the march to help Aiken continue on with the struggle."

"And just where you gone stay? At the Wilbridge Inn?" Mr. Brown guffawed, egging on a number of others.

"Now, Bill." Pastor Bell stood up. "There is no need for that kind of talk. Mr. Pennington is our guest. Let him talk."

"Thank you, Pastor Bell," said Pennington. "I can take it from here." The Pastor sat back down hesitantly, not altogether reassured.

"I understand your concerns, Mr. Brown," said Pennington. "May I speak honestly?" He waited until Mr. Brown nodded reluctantly and then continued. "The fact is, I was hoping that some of you kind people would be willing to open up your homes to us for a few weeks." There was some murmuring in the congregation. "The community in Charlotte helped us out and it worked beautifully. Don't forget that next weekend Aiken is going to have almost every newspaper in the nation here covering the President's visit. I know he is supposed to be here to announce and garner support for Mayor Stanton's run for the Senate, but my sources tell me that the President's speech will announce sweeping changes in the government. Rumor has it that the federal government is going to have to enforce laws to allow you to vie for federal jobs and programs that are rightfully yours."

"What about us women?" Lillian called up to the man on the dais. "Will he address women's rights?"

No one in the congregation was surprised at this outburst, but for a brief moment, Mr. Pennington, known for his cool calm, looked flustered. To give him credit, he recovered quickly. "Why yes, yes, I believe he will." He took a good look at the woman who had spoken up, put off not as much by her gender, but by the fact that she was a black woman willing to speak her mind, and in church.

Lillian seized her chance. "Don't you think we need to appoint someone to meet with the First Lady, Mr. Pennington? She has shown herself to be sympathetic to the cause, and to allowing the vote for women."

Mr. Pennington nodded along with many of the women, but was saved from a direct response by Mr. Carter, a church deacon. "Even if we protest," he said, "those reporters aren't coming on our side of town anyway. There'll be no one to protest to."

Mr. Pennington would not be dissuaded, however. "That's exactly why I propose we head for Whiskey Road. The Wilbridge Inn. The Blue Landing Club. Everywhere a function is planned, that's where we need to be."

"You are not asking us to march. You all are asking for an all-out riot!" yelled Mr. Smith, another outspoken deacon.

Suddenly, the murmuring in the crowd grew to a dull roar. The congregation was dividing.

"No, no, no. Think about it," Pennington called out over the congregation, trying to regain order. "There will be all kinds of dignitaries. And the President of the United States!"

The room quieted a bit. "Mr. Pennington, let's be honest here." Mr. Brown stepped forward. "Do you really think they are gone let us get anywhere near any of those places? We'd be seen as a threat to the President just for walking by. No telling how many of us would be shot dead."

"Maybe in the past," said Pennington with fervor. "But this is a different time and a different situation. With reporters from all over the country—even the world—here, do you think those in power in Aiken want to be seen shooting innocent people?

"I think Mr. Pennington has a point," Lillian called out. She liked the way this man thought and wanted everyone to know it—although the look he gave her appeared suspiciously cool.

"The popularity of the radio all but ensures that we will have a live feed," the white man went on. "You all even have a radio station in Columbia now." He held up his hands as a few people began to talk at once and waited until they quieted. "Look. I'm not saying we do anything radical that would get any of us killed. I'm just saying we show up at every venue with signs in tow and request a meeting to hand over our concerns about the treatment of Negroes down here in the south. It's not going to work if there are only a few dozen of us. They'll call us crazies. But if we show up in numbers and organized, they'll have to take us seriously. And if they refuse to give us a meeting, the world will know that things are not right. Sure, there are some progressive programs on the books, but until they are enforced to benefit everyone, they might as well be null and void. That's what we are aiming to do—make them enforce the laws that are already on the books."

Lillian stood up. "I think we should do it," she said. "You can count me in, Mr. Pennington." She looked around as if daring the others to join her. "Do you really think there are a hundred others who will join us?"

"I can guarantee at least that number," said Pennington, "including our lawyers and all the officers. If you add that to the local population, we should have at least a couple hundred concerned citizens turn out."

"That's pretty good for Aiken," said Lillian.

"Think about the potential." Pennington was feeding off Lillian's positive energy. "No sitting president has had to deal with colored protestors in the history of this nation. Just think about what kind of a statement that would make."

"I do have one question," interjected Pastor Bell. "How do you propose to get a list of grievances to the President if you can't even get within a few feet of him? Not to mention the fact that Bull and his boys will probably have barriers set to keep us away from that side of town."

"Excuse me? Bull? And who?"

"Sheriff Bull Baker and his hateful band of brothers."

Pennington nodded. "The WWO. As long as we keep our plans under wraps, we can surprise them. They can't stop over two hundred people." He waited until the group had settled again and then said, "Every last one of us needs to be prepared to show up at every event all weekend long. We'll work out a system for breaks, but we need to commit to the long haul. About how many men are active in the WWO in these parts?"

"That's hard to say," grumbled Mike Clark, a big man with an even bigger bass voice. "They usually like to travel in packs of around ten or fifteen."

There were nods from the congregation.

"Imagine their surprise when they see our numbers, then!" said Pennington enthusiastically. "Imagine how unprepared they'll be. And even if they do have a plan, they only have a certain number of men to cover an entire weekend of events that will take place all over town. Surely we can overwhelm two or three hate mongers at a time. If they do try to get the word out to other communities, by the time anyone travels to Aiken, the weekend will be over. We will have made our point two or three times over."

"We have our own group who can take on the WWO," said Deacon Fryer. "Jake Freeman and his boys."

Mr. Brown was on his feet in a hot second. "Deacon Fryer, I'm surprised at you! Jake Freeman! That man does the devil's work! You can't trust a man like that to protect God's children in their hour of need!" he yelled.

The congregation set to mumbling, some in agreement, some not sure. They looked to Pastor Bell for his words of wisdom.

Meanwhile, Goldie sat frozen in her seat, desperately making the attempt to keep her face emotionless, while in her mind she imagined defending her man in a voice as loud and strong as her mamma's. Why, a man like Mr. Brown had no knowledge of how much Jake had to pay Bull and his boys to look the other way when patrons made their wobbly treks home. But instead she sat there, cold and stiff, feeling as if all the eyes of the church were upon her.

"Simmer down, now," said the pastor, "simmer down. It's no good arguing amongst us. We all know that Jake Freeman and his boys run a speakeasy, and we all know that some of the righteous in this very church frequent that speakeasy from time to time." He paused to let his words sink in.

"A speakeasy is one thing, Pastor. But what about all that other stuff?" demanded Mr. Brown.

"And what about all those stories we hear about the goings-on there and about the things Jake Freeman's done?" Johnnie Flower added.

"Now, church, it sure sounds like a lot of gossip to me, and y'all know how I feel about gossip and rumors. I personally don't know if any of those things are true about Jake Freeman. And until any of you do know firsthand...." Pastor Bell waited. He knew not an individual in his church would confess seeing the "goings on" in Jake's club, let alone that they'd been there. He nodded. "Then, I would suggest we assume they are nothing more than rumors. Don't forget that just a few years ago nightclubs were legal—not that such places were any less sinful. However, I do not believe in condemning Jake Freeman simply because he owns such a club. Therefore, if he is so inclined to lend us the use of his men to keep this beloved congregation safe, I say we humbly accept."

. . .

After a moment of silence while the parishioners considered the pastor's strong endorsement, Jason Washington said, "That all sounds good in theory, Pastor, but how does Mr. Pennington here intend to ensure our grievances reach the President of the United States?"

Lillian could not be restrained. "His wife, of course! She has his ear every night."

Again Winthrop Pennington looked at Lillian, but this time with far more interest. "That's a good point, Mrs—?"

"Jackson. Lillian Jackson."

"That's a good point, Mrs. Jackson. I have here a list of grievances and recommendations for policy and enforcement to hand over to the President, but your suggestion to share them with Mrs. Jameson is well taken."

"And to the press," Lillian said. "They should have our demands in writing so there's no misunderstanding."

"I like it," Pennington nodded, wondering if the attractive woman with the gift for debate was married. "For discretion's sake, however, we will keep our written list covert until the time comes, given the close vicinity of the WWO. The only way we will succeed is through the element of surprise."

Soon the pastor was sending around a piece of paper to gather names of those willing and able to take in members of the NCRO, who would arrive that Thursday afternoon. Moments later, he was leading the congregation in a final prayer and then dismissing them home for Sunday supper.

. . .

Lillian and her girls were animatedly reviewing the meeting and the presence of a white man in their church when Mr. Pennington caught up with them on the church steps.

"Mrs. Jackson!"

Lillian turned, surprised. "Mr. Pennington. How may I help you?"

"I see your name here on the list. You and your husband's name, actually."

Lillian blushed. "I'm afraid that must be an old list, then. My husband was killed by the WWO a while back."

It was Pennington's turn to flush. "I'm so sorry, Mrs. Jackson. I had no idea."

Lillian gave a dignified nod. "You had no way of knowing."

"I...I was going to ask if you might have, well, if it wouldn't be too much trouble, that I might stay at your place, but under the circumstances...." Pennington was flushing, unaccustomed to embarrassment.

Lillian's shoulders went back. "You are most welcome, Mr. Pennington. My girls and I will expect you. Good day."

"Good day, then, Mrs. Jackson," said Pennington, agape at Lillian's poise.

This weekend was sure to change the lives of everyone in Aiken. Perhaps the country.

Chapter 15

"It sounds like our Mr. Pennington was already sweet on Grandma Lillian," said Shelby.

"Well, why wouldn't he be? We had the prettiest mamma in South Carolina," said Rose.

"That's right," said Goldie. "Where do you think we got our good looks, or you got yours, for that matter?"

Shelby grinned. "So what happened—with Grandmamma and Mr. Pennington, I mean?"

"We'll get to that later," Rose said. "There was so much that happened that week, it's hard to know exactly where to start."

"For one," said Goldie, "Mamma had forbidden me to see Jake. The day I stood up to her was one of the most difficult of my life. But Mamma had to know that I was no longer her little girl, that as a woman I had a right to make my own decisions on matters of the heart."

"Grandmamma doesn't sound like someone who got stood up to very often," Shelby commented drily.

"Well, no." Goldie admitted. "But she was my mother."

. . .

It was Monday afternoon, only days before Mr. Pennington and his colleagues from the NCRO would arrive. Goldie had just gotten in from school and was dropping off her things before she left for the Stantons'.

"Goldie, I need to talk to you before you leave for work."

"Okay, Mamma, but you know I can't afford to be late."

Lillian nodded and patted the sofa next to her.

Goldie sat down, worried. Did her mother know about Jake, about how they were meeting in secret? Would Goldie try to deny it?

"I'm going to be honest with you," Lillian started, "which is more than I can say for you."

Goldie blanched. Her secret was out. Her mother knew.

Lillian sighed a huge sigh, letting Goldie know just how disappointed her mother was in her older daughter.

"There is a lot going on this week, what with the NCRO people coming and the goings-on this weekend."

What? Wasn't her mother going to demand she stop seeing Jake? This was unexpected.

"The fact is that once word gets out about my involvement, I will become a target for the WWO, just like your daddy."

"Mamma, no! Don't talk like that."

"Goldie, hear me out. If you are grown up enough to make the decision to keep company with a man like Jake Freeman, you are grown up enough to hear what I have to say." Lillian took Goldie's hand. "You know that I do not approve of your seeing him. I am smart enough to know, however, that my opinions of the man will most certainly only make his arms that much more enticing." Again, Goldie went to argue, but her mother cut her off. "Having said that, and going against my morals, I feel it is necessary to swallow my pride and ask for Jake's help."

Goldie's mouth dropped open straight down to her knees.

"I need to keep this family safe," Lillan went on. "I can't do that alone. I must ask you to ask Jake to assign a couple of his men to our house. It's not me I'm worried about. But if anything happened to you or Rose, why—I—"

"Nothin's going to happen, Mamma!" Goldie protested. "And, Mamma, I am so very sorry for going behind your back. But I love him, Mamma, and if you forbade me to see him, then I—"

"Stop, Goldie. I know. But please understand."

"Understand what?"

"Understand that there is something I must ask you to do."

Goldie had a bad feeling about what was coming. Sure enough, the hammer fell.

"I need you to stop seeing Jake—at least for a while," Lillian said.

Goldie gulped. "S—stop seeing him? But, why? For how long?"

"As long as it takes. The next few days will be dangerous for all of us. You know as I do that Jake Freeman will be right in the middle of it."

"But Mamma, Jake wouldn't let anything happen to me. Why, you're asking for his help! Why do I need to stop seeing him?"

"Sweetie, weren't you listening to me?" Lillian cupped Goldie's face in her hands to look directly into her daughter's eyes.

Goldie felt as if the air had gone out of her. "Yes, I was listening. I suppose...I suppose I understand. But only if it's just for the week, Mamma." Goldie knew her voice lacked conviction.

"A week will not be nearly long enough, Goldie. And you know it."

Goldie waited, already seeing the days without Jake in them stretching endlessly out before her.

"This week is just the tip of the iceberg, Goldie, and it's radical. More than likely there will be those who will lose their lives in the fight. They will not hold back in cracking down on anyone involved in the march, Jake included. He represents too much power for coloreds. Knocking him down would send a deliberate message to colored folk to stay in their place. I don't want you caught in the middle. If the WWO know that you and Jake are...together... nothing will give them greater pleasure than returning to this house, to this family, and unleashing more of their anger."

Goldie shook her head back and forth, unwilling to accept the truth.

"You know I'm right, Goldie. And don't forget who you work for. You are dating the mayor's nemesis, and you are the daughter of a woman who is going to cause him a considerable amount of hell."

"But, Mamma, the Stantons don't know that Jake and I—"

"Goldie," Lillian paused to remind herself that Goldie was still young and naive when it came to some matters of the world. "Aiken is a small town. Don't think for one minute that Bull Baker does not have eyes and ears at Nate's place. Bull is all too familiar with Jake and the workings of his business, and you'd be stupid to pretend otherwise. Besides, you don't think a drunk would give you up to get out of jail?"

Goldie had no argument for that.

"Even after this weekend, there is going to be a lot of debate about Prohibition. Jake will be plenty busy dealing with those issues. Baby, if it is meant to be, it will be. If you two are meant to be together, whether it takes a few days or a few months, so you will be. When you see Jake, you need to tell him that you must not be seen in his company for a while. Tell him if he really cares about you, he will understand and let you be, as well as spare a few able-bodied men during these trying times."

. . .

Though it was only three hours until she would be with Jake again, this was to be the longest night Goldie had ever experienced.

Each second cleaning silver, making beds, and arranging the cupboards to ready for the Stantons' guests dragged by like the sun going down on a hot summer's day. She went over and over the conversation she'd had with her mamma, praying that asking Jake to help her family with protection meant her mamma would soften to him over time.

Goldie often daydreamed at work, imagining she and Jake lived at Manhattan, but tonight the smell of magnolias was soon replaced by cooking grease. And the gowns in her mind held nothing in common with the plain uniform and apron she wore every day.

Miss Mable was managing the kitchen tonight and she had pulled Goldie's head to her bosom upon her arrival. "There you are, baby," she said. "I was getting worried. Is everything all right?" She gave Goldie a look that was far too piercing for comfort.

"Everything's fine, Miss Mable, just fine."

Unconvinced but in a hurry, Miss Mable allowed Goldie to drop the subject. "She wants you to prep in the kitchen tonight."

Goldie groaned. She despised prep work, preferring to work around the house. That way, she was more susceptible to hear some nugget of information she could take to Jake.

"'Nuff o' that, young lady. If you want yo' job, you'll get yourself in that kitchen right now!" Miss Mable pointed her finger in the direction of the work area, her massive body shaking with every word she spoke. "You can start with those potatoes," she added with her usual bluster. She handed Goldie the peeler.

Laura Bell, Caroline Stanton's head assistant, laughed and left the kitchen, being summoned by the queen herself. "Her royalty calls," Goldie wiseacred and proceeded to waltz through the room imitating her employer, the mayor's wife. Sure enough, it wasn't long before Goldie was also heralded to join Laura in Caroline Stanton's suite.

Outside her door, Goldie heard the soothing voices of the maids and Caroline Stanton's high, shrill staccato. "The Granberrys! From New York! They'll be here any minute."

Goldie knocked and stepped over the threshold.

"Goldie," said Mrs. Stanton icily. "What took you so long? Come on in here, girl!"

"Yes, ma'am."

"Help Laura Bell lay out my unmentionables and my dress. No. No. I need you to paint my nails instead."

"Yes, ma'am." Goldie rushed to her employer's armoire to pick up the tray of nail lacquer so she could choose a color.

Goldie knew that Miss Caroline would choose the brightest red in the set. Any other place a color like that might not be such a big deal, but down here in Aiken, South Carolina, there were certain things ladies did not do, especially ones with old money. Goldie had to give Caroline points for that, at least. She didn't care what the other ladies thought of her. She relished that they envied her from top to bottom and wanted to keep it that way.

"And take out the matching lipstick."

"Yes, ma'am."

Goldie had just sat down to paint Miss Caroline's nails when her sister Julia arrived.

"Ooh, Caroline, what a divine color! It's my turn next."

"Just as soon as Goldie is finished."

Goldie hoped it would not take too long. And she did not appreciate being loaned to Julia, a woman with far too much time on her hands and nothing to fill it with, in Goldie's opinion.

Julia took in Goldie from top to bottom. "You certainly have some attractive help," she commented. "Don't you ever get worried?"

Goldie could not believe the woman was two feet away, but speaking about her as if the "help" didn't have ears. She prayed Julie's word wouldn't cause Mrs. Stanton to focus on regrettable topics.

"I've heard plenty of stories about southern men and their help," Julia pressed, raising her eyebrows.

"You seem to have forgotten, my dear," Caroline said loftily, "My Zach is not a southerner."

"Oh, I don't know," Julia said, examining her nails, "he's already reinvented himself to run as a South Carolina senator. You can't get more southern than that."

"Hush now, Julia," Caroline snapped. Why was Julia always butting into her affairs? "Why don't you get married already? Then you won't have so much time to worry about me."

"I'm having too much fun as it is, that's why. I've got my career and my driver's license. What more do I need?"

"You wouldn't have to change anything to get married."

Julia curled her lip. "Really? Look at you! You were supposed to get your advanced degree in education and be a college professor."

Caroline was defensive. "You're right. But that's a choice I made. I did not have to give up the pursuit of a collegiate career. Believe it or not, there are several prominent universities here in South Carolina."

"Oh, my. Looks like I've struck a nerve."

"I don't think so, dear. I'm simply stating the facts."

Goldie finished Miss Caroline's nails. Julia and her sister traded seats. Julia held out her hands for Goldie to begin. "Well, I guess you can't work full time and be the First Lady, too," she conceded.

"Oh, please," said Caroline, but she looked pleased.

"Don't tell me you and Zach haven't discussed it."

Suddenly, Caroline seemed to remember there were others in the room. "Let's drop the matter, shall we?" she said abruptly.

"Come on, Sis. If Zach gets elected to the Senate as one of the youngest members in history, he would be groomed for the presidency and you know it."

"Well...." said Caroline. "The thought had crossed my mind."

That sent the sisters into a fit of giggles and Julia's hand would have upset the nail lacquer if Goldie hadn't been watching so carefully. In setting it right, she gripped Julia's hand tightly.

Julia gave Goldie a look that bore a hole right through her. Sensing she'd better play her cards right, Goldie looked down fast, but Julia wasn't a fool. Goldie could only hope Miss Caroline's sister had not seen the anger—and fear—in Goldie's own eyes.

Mrs. Stanton needed the help of two girls to get dressed. The outfit would have looked better on Goldie, but that was scant comfort. Goldie quietly and efficiently performed her tasks, keeping an eye on the clock as she did.

But Caroline Stanton was not done with her. She often found extra work for Goldie to compensate for her husband's evident favoritism. Tonight it was cleaning the mayor's study, even though there were only ten minutes left on Goldie's shift.

. . .

As Goldie neared the study, she saw the door was partly open. The voices of Bull Baker and Mayor Stanton could clearly be heard. Instead of knocking and entering, she crept up as close to the door as possible to put her ear to the door. She would do anything to help her man.

Chapter 16

"Sheriff, have you talked to Jake Freeman yet?"

Goldie's heart immediately set to racing.

"I plan to pay him a visit tomorrow."

"Do you have the places around town covered where my guests will convene?"

"It's all taken care of."

A few seconds went by. Then, "Here's a copy of the itinerary for the weekend."

Goldie almost jumped for joy. She had to get her hands on one of those itineraries to help her mother and Mr. Pennington. A drawer closed with a thump. The mayor must be keeping them in his desk.

"There's one other matter, Sheriff. I've decided to take action on that bit of information you shared with me recently. You remember. About how Jake Freeman's source for libations is the same as mine?"

The sheriff grunted.

"Well, instead of letting my club manager handle the delivery this Thursday night, I will be there to oversee it personally. I've rescheduled the delivery day, which will now take place the same night as the ball. It's a perfect scenario. Everyone will be there watching when I personally catch the biggest gangster that Aiken has ever seen."

The biggest gangster Aiken had ever seen? Jake Freeman? "Now, why in the hell would you do a damn fool thing like that?" asked the sheriff.

"I did some checking, Sheriff. I know that Jake's drop is directly after mine."

"Hell, I told you that."

"I beg to differ," said the mayor. "And you certainly didn't tell me that he uses my drop zone as well."

Bull scratched his head and sighed.

"I've arranged for an anonymous tip to the press and the feds to ensure they'll be there to catch Freeman red-handed."

The sheriff again declined to answer.

"You were dragging your feet on the matter, Sheriff. I cannot have Jake Freeman ruining my weekend. This will prove I have no qualms working with the federal government to enforce national laws. But my plan is even more brilliant. Nabbing Freeman also shows devout South Carolina National Federal Party and the National State Party members that I am willing to come down hard on anyone who breaks the law."

The sheriff was confused. "Why would you want to impress the National State Party when you're on the National Federal Party ticket?"

"My, oh my," said the mayor. "I do forget sometimes that you're not particularly savvy politically. Obviously, I need to come off as a moderate to the good ol' National Federal Party if I want to accomplish my goals."

The mayor sure was condescending to the sheriff, thought Goldie.

"So, let me get this straight," said Bull. "You're willing to come down on anyone who happens to be colored—'enforce the law,' as you say—to impress National Federal Party bigwigs up north. At the same time you'll be nabbing one of the most arrogant coloreds we got just to prove to us country white folk down here that you ain't like those other Yankees. That about cover it?"

"Good for you, Bull," said the mayor like a proud teacher.

"What if your plan backfires?" asked Bull, shaking his head. "If the feds catch you runnin' rum, Jake Freeman or not, they'll come after yo' ass soon as they're finished with him."

"I am purchasing only the finest liquors and wines to serve the President of the United States of America," the mayor said. "It would be breaking the law to serve him local hooch or whatever the hell you people make."

"There you go again," said Bull sullenly, "with the generalizin'."

"You know I'm right or you wouldn't be riding my coattails trying to catch a few crumbs," the mayor said.

Just then there was a knock at the door.

. . .

"Goldie!" The mayor glanced at his wristwatch. "Isn't it a little late for you to be here?"

"Excuse me, Mayor Stanton, sir, but Mrs. Stanton told me to come clean this room before I leave for the night."

Bull sent Goldie a suspicious glance. She studiously avoided his eyes. Did he suspect her of listening?

"Goldie, the sheriff and I are conducting business in here tonight. You may clean it tomorrow."

"Goldie?"

It was Mrs. Stanton, come to check on Goldie.

"Where are you? Have you finished cleaning? Don't go until that study is spick and span."

The mayor's wife came into view. She gave a brief nod of distain at the sheriff.

"I've told Goldie to head on home, my dear. Bull and I have business to attend to. She can do it tomorrow."

"You mean all this time—?" Caroline scowled at Goldie, then remembered scowling produced wrinkles and smoothed out her facial muscles.

Before another word could be spoken, Goldie rushed out the door. "Yes, sir. Good evening, sir. Ma'am."

Bull left shortly thereafter. The Stantons were left looking at each other with, as usual, nothing much to say.

. . .

Goldie stepped inside Nate's club, closed the door behind her, and breathed a sigh of relief. What if she'd been caught? What if the mayor guessed she'd been eavesdropping at his door? The consequences were too terrible to entertain. She spotted Jake across the room and was wrapped in his embrace in seconds.

"Goldie, you could have been discovered!" Jake said when she told him what she'd done. "What were you thinking! I told you to stop this interfering."

"Don't worry," Goldie said, but she couldn't look him in the eye. "No one saw me. Besides, the mayor told the sheriff that he's called in the feds to catch you red-handed when the delivery comes."

"...And look the other way while Stanton gets his, I would imagine," protested Jake, "given the mayor will be serving the President of the United States. But who am I foolin'? Even if he weren't serving the President, he's still the mayor. And he's still white."

"So you'll stop the delivery?" Goldie pushed hopefully.

Jake shook his head. "Goldie, you know I can't do that. I have too many people depending on me."

"Can't you skip just this one delivery?" pleaded Goldie.

"There's always another way," said Jake, "and I plan to find it."

Goldie felt tears coming on.

"Come on, honey, don't be like that. I appreciate your help, but from now on you need to stay out of these affairs. Things are getting far too dangerous, and I couldn't live with myself if anything happened to you because of me."

"I can take care of myself," said Goldie, affronted.

But Jake wouldn't give. "Goldie, I mean it. Stay out of it. It's time you let me handle things. And stop snooping around Manhattan."

Goldie nodded, her fingers tightly crossed behind her back.

. . .

When she got home, Jasper, one of Jake's men, stepped from the shadows to relieve Isaac, who had walked Goldie home. The men said their goodnights and waited until Goldie Jackson had disappeared into the house before conversing.

"How much longer do we think we'll be on this detail?" Jasper complained.

"Long as the boss wants us on it," said Isaac. "'Sides, what difference does it make? You gettin' the same paycheck no matter what you do."

Jasper harrumphed. He'd rather be working in the bar, where there was always the chance for a little nip or two.

"You don't get paid to think, neither," said Isaac. "Now, go ahead, get yo' ass back to the club. And bring me back something to drink and eat. It's time to start 'spectin' your elders."

Jasper sidled away, mumbling about the unfairness of his position, leaving Isaac, Jake's loyal friend and employee, to watch over the Jackson household another night.

Chapter 17

"But what happened to the sheriff, Mamma?" Shelby wanted to know.

"Sheriff Bull Baker might not have been the brightest bulb in the box, but he knew what he was doing when it came to his job," said Goldie.

"But what did he do?" Shelby insisted.

"Followed your mamma back to the club and spied on her with Jake, that's what," said Goldie. "He knew his suspicions were right when he saw Goldie in Jake's arms. The sheriff knew without a doubt that she was telling him what she'd overhead between the mayor and himself.

"But, even more importantly, now he knew that they were lovers."

. . .

When Bull got up the next morning, he headed straight for the mayor's office. He skipped the big breakfast that Laney made for him every morning, her disapproval at his back. He even bypassed Clem's store. The local gossip didn't hold a candle to the information he had.

Truth be told, Bull had been divided on ratting out the Jackson girl, who was no longer a girl, apparently, but Jake Freeman's lover. And a spy! He had always considered the family of Denver Jackson to be on the straight and narrow; the girls to be good nigra girls. But this one had sure taken a wrong turn.

The sheriff didn't want anything bad to happen to Goldie, but if she was mixed up with the likes of Jake Freeman, it was out of his hands.

Then, next thing you know, without a thought in his head about it, Bull had reversed direction. Five minutes later, he found himself on Lillian Jackson's porch. What he was doing there, he hardly knew. He usually avoided the woman, his guilt over the death of her husband keeping him far from her sight. He felt the stares of the neighbors as he shifted from foot to foot, probably wondering like he was what in the name of tarnation he was doing there, somewhere he was welcome about as much as a bad case of poison ivy.

Bull knocked and braced himself for Lillian's wrath. This was one woman unafraid of the sheriff or any other white since they'd stolen her Denver.

Goldie answered the door. Surprised, they stared at each other for a moment. Bull had expected the girls to be on their way to school already. He squinted at her to see if he could pick up the guile in her eyes, but all he saw were big brown circles in a creamy-skinned face.

"Sheriff Baker. What are you doing here?"

"Mornin', Goldie," said the sheriff, attempting to recover. "I'm here to speak with your mother."

"Goldie, who's at the door?" Lillian stepped into view. "Why, Sheriff," she said. The ice in her voice could have frozen the fur off a polar bear. "To what do we owe this honor?"

"I know I'm not welcome, ma'am, and I don't mean you no harm. I just need to have a few words with you. Alone, if you don't mind."

"Well, you don't have to worry about that, do you, now that my Denver is dead."

Bull went white, if a white man could be said to get much paler.

"Miss Lillian, I meant the girls. Aren't they supposed to be on their way to school?"

"We can go late, Mamma," said Rose from a few feet behind her mother.

"No, you girls get on to school," insisted Lillian, curiosity getting the better of her. "I'll be fine. I'm sure the sheriff doesn't mean to hurt me. Isn't that right, Sheriff?"

Bull nodded, feeling shameful down to his toes.

"Are you sure, Mamma?" Goldie asked.

"Yes. Now go ahead or you'll be late."

The girls left, casting long glances back to the house until they were out of sight.

"We can talk out here on the porch," instructed Lillian.

"I'd prefer to have this conversation inside, if you don't mind," said Bull.

"I do mind," said Lillian. "Either talk to me out here or we don't talk at all."

Bull conceded, but was concerned about how it would look. If word got out that he was warning the Jacksons, his name would be mud around Aiken. Even the appearance of sympathy on his part would be detrimental to his reputation. "All right, Lillian, all right. You drive a hard bargain."

"Well, then, spit it out. I don't have all day."

Bull nodded and spoke quietly. "I don't like having to bring you this kind of news, Lillian, but I feel I must."

"News? Was it any easier to tell me that you all had murdered my husband, Sheriff? What's so important you have to come to my home to tell me?"

"I know you're angry, Lillian, I know. It's just that Goldie—" he watched Lillian's eyes grow big and round "—well, I'm just gonna say it. Your Goldie's been seeing that Jake Freeman character. And I gotta tell ya, I'm…disappointed."

Lillian's reaction surprised Bull, who'd expected horror or, at the very least, dismay. Instead, she laughed.

"You mean to tell me you came all the way out here to tell me how bad you feel that my daughter is seein' Jake Freeman?"

Bull pulled at his collar. "Forget about how I feel, then. Your husband was a decent man. This Jake character ain't a good influence. And let's just say he won't be around for too much longer. 'Sides, your family done already suffered a loss."

"You think I need you to remind me of that?" Lillian raised her voice in anger.

"No, no, course not," said Bull, realizing his blunder. "But if Goldie keeps messin' around with Freeman, she could find herself in a whole heap a trouble."

"I'm sure that's just your guilt talking, Bull."

"Now, Miss Lillian, I came here to do the right thing…to help you with your little girl."

"Right," said Lillian sarcastically. "I tell you what, Sheriff. Why don't you let me worry about my girls and you worry about your boys."

"But I was just trying to—"

"I know exactly," interrupted Lillian, "what you are trying to do, Sheriff. And I don't appreciate it one bit. Now, if you don't mind, I got work to do."

Bull thanked Lillian Jackson for her time, but she'd already gone back inside.

Things were looking bad for the sheriff of Aiken. Real bad.

Chapter 18

As Bull Baker neared Mayor Stanton's office, he thought about his less than satisfying conversation with Lillian Jackson. But now, instead of feeling guilty and ashamed, he felt angry and belittled. Damn nigra was too damn proud for her own good. If Lillian's daughter found trouble messin' 'round with Jake Freeman, she'd get what she deserved. Wasn't his business. He'd warned them, and that was more than he should have done.

In control once more, he entered the mayor's inner sanctum. Adeline was there, and noticeably less sullen than usual. "Morning, Sheriff Baker. Isn't it excitin'? The President of the United States right here in Aiken!"

Bull nodded.

"I just wish my Alton was here to see it all. That man was the picture of—"

"He sure was, Adeline," Bull agreed, cutting her off before she went on one of her famous Alton-in-all-his-glory tirades, "but I need to see the mayor. Is he in?"

"He's just finishing up with Mrs. Roland," said Adeline, dabbing her tears with the ever-present tissue she'd kept in her sleeve for as long as Bull had known her.

Just as he was about to knock, Mrs. Roland opened the door on her way out.

"Mrs. Roland. How you doin' this mornin'?" Bull said.

"Fine, thank you, Sheriff. You?" She didn't wait for an answer. "And call me Lena."

Bull nodded.

"How's that little wife of yours?" asked Betty Jean, eyes all squinty.

"Laney's fine, thanks for asking," said Bull.

"You tell her I'll be gettin' back in touch with her real soon, y' hear?"

They both knew the likes of Mrs. Roland would never in a million years socialize with the likes of the sheriff's wife, but Bull nodded and smiled, as etiquette dictated. Before he had time to say another word, Mrs. Roland was already half way across the room. She'd cut him off without thinking about it twice. He shrugged, used to being snubbed by the upper crust, and went through the door.

"Knock, knock." Bull tapped on Stanton's guest chair and sat down.

"I guess you read my mind, Bull. We have some things to finalize, but it seems you've been doing your job."

"I aim to please," said Bull. "However, there is something I think you should hear."

The mayor put down the papers in his hand and pursed his lips. "I'm waiting."

"Well, you know that gal that works for you—Goldie Jackson?"

"'Course I do. She's been a good little worker right from the start."

"But did you know that this 'good little worker' has been messin' around with Jake Freeman?"

"No," said the mayor flatly. "I don't believe it."

"It's true. I saw them with my own eyes."

"Really? What exactly did you see? Why don't you tell me, Sheriff?"

"After she left your house the other night—you know, after we had our little discussion?—she hightailed it directly on over to Nate's. I followed her."

"So? All the coloreds go to Nate's. That means nothing. You should know better than to bring me something like that, Bull."

Bull couldn't help it. He smirked. "You think that little girl's goin' there to cut a rug, Mayor? What I saw says otherwise."

"I'm still waiting," said Stanton, drumming his fingers on the desk top.

"That Goldie Jackson was cozy as all get-out with Freeman—and I mean in that particular way, iffen you catch my drift. Then one of his goons walked her home."

"I see."

Bull watched as Stanton's wheels turned to process the news.

The sheriff was pleased with his ability to turn the tables. "How do you want me to handle her, then? There ain't no tellin' what she heard that night when we were talking—or at other times, for that matter—and took back to Jake."

"I'll have to percolate on this for a while, Bull."

"Don't have much time, Mayor. I'll be happy to handle it for you."

"No!"

The mayor's outburst was surprising, but Bull let it go. Something would have to be done soon enough. They both knew it.

He got back to the President's visit. "I've deputized several men for tomorrow." Bull handed the list to Stanton.

"I assume these gentlemen are close, personal friends of yours?"

"Pardon?"

"You know what I mean. Are they members of the WWO?"

"Excuse me!"

"Listen, don't get all huffy on me. Your associates have a tendency to get sloppy in their dealings, as you are well aware."

"You won't just let it go, will ya'?" Apparently, the mayor would never stop referring to the Denver Jackson situation.

"Look at it from my point of view, Bull. I cannot have a bunch of thugs—some might even say murderers—around the President of the United States and other dignitaries. The feds are there to protect him, but coloreds and whites'll be out en masse to try to catch a glimpse of him. We cannot afford clashes of any kind between the coloreds and your associates."

"My men know how to be professional."

"I'm counting on you to make sure of that, Bull. Don't disappoint me."

"Yes, sir," Bull said sullenly.

"Just in case there are any problems, which I am sure there will not be," Stanton went on, "I have asked Sheriff Moody from Columbia to come down and help out with a few of his best trained men. Who knows, they may even teach your boys a thing or two."

Sonovabitch. "How dare you bring another sheriff into my jurisdiction?" yelled Bull. "Bad enough I got to deal with the damn feds. Now you're bringing in Moody?"

Stanton remained calm. "It's nothing personal, Bull. I'm sure you can see that. I'm doing this for your future as well. Wouldn't a nice security detail in Columbia or even Washington D.C. be amenable at some point? Hell, you could be one of those damn feds yourself."

"I don't like it. Not one damn bit, Stanton."

"Well, it doesn't really matter what you like or don't like, Sheriff. I think you know that by now. Am I right?"

It felt as if the temperature in the room had suddenly dropped twenty degrees.

Bull surely did know where he stood.

"Good," said the mayor. "Moving along, then. When the President's train arrives tomorrow at noon, I will be there with you and your deputies. Sheriff Moody will escort the President to the Wilbridge Inn."

Bull was bristling, but nodded.

"And your pals will not get anywhere near the President. Is that clear? They are strictly to monitor the coloreds and keep them in check. Capisce?"

"Sure." Whatever that means.

"You are personally on duty all weekend."

"I figured as much. I'll stay until he goes down for the night."

"No. I have made arrangements for you at the Wilbridge as well."

"But it's all booked up," Bull protested.

"There's room for a cot in the office where the workers get ready for work."

"You mean where the coloreds get ready? You've got to be kidding." Bull was outraged.

"No kidding here, Bull. We all have our cross to bear in these difficult times. 'Course, if you'd rather I get someone else, like Sheriff Moody, I can do that."

"That won't be necessary." Bull said tightly.

"Good. Now, is there anything else we need to cover? Because I need to finish working on my speech."

When Bull left, the mayor was already thinking about how to get back at Jake Freeman for consorting with the woman of his dreams.

Chapter 19

Goldie sensed the change in the mayor as soon as she stepped into Manhattan that day. Mrs. Stanton was on her way to the beauty shop with her sister to gussy up for all the upcoming parties. Besides the rest of the help, Goldie and the mayor had the house to themselves, a fact which already had the hairs on the back of her neck standing at attention. Something was up, she just didn't know what.

The help lived by an unwritten law that clearly stated that no one was to put his or her job on the line to help another worker. You did that, your job—and your life—was at stake. Goldie lived according to that law along with everybody else. Even if a colored woman was raped by a white man, there was nothing that could be done about. You learned early on to keep your mouth shut. Not that Goldie was afraid of the mayor. Not really.

Still, her anxiety was high as a kite.

"Good afternoon, Mayor," she said politely. "Mrs. Stanton left a list for me. She wanted me to start with your office. But I see you're busy. I can come back when you're done."

"No. Goldie, that won't be necessary. I could use the company, and your input on my speech. For a colored girl, you really are quite bright."

Goldie bit back a retort, feeling fear in the pit of her stomach. "Oh no, sir, I couldn't do that. I have my duties to attend to."

"I wasn't asking, Goldie."

Goldie went still.

"You don't plan to disobey a direct order from your employer, Goldie, do you?"

"No, sir," Goldie said miserably. She sat down in the plush leather seat in front of the mayor's desk and catty corner to the huge picture window.

Mayor Stanton noted how the rays of the sun made a halo around the girl's head and gave her whole body a glow.

"Mayor Stanton, please, I really don't feel comfortable leaving my work for Miss Mable to do. She has a bad back. So, if you don't mind—"

"Essie Mae can do it, then. There. Do you feel better now?"

The queasy feeling in Goldie's gut worsened, but she nodded in agreement as she was expected to.

"Goldie, are you aware that I'll be making a big announcement in front of some very important people this weekend?"

Goldie nodded reluctantly. Where was the mayor going with this line of questioning? Did saying yes indicate that she'd heard things she shouldn't have?

"That's right. And if all goes well, you'll be able to say you once worked for a United States Senator someday, maybe even a president."

Goldie strained to appear pleased. It felt as if she were grimacing.

"That's unless you would like to continue working for me in a more private capacity—perhaps as my secretary or private teacher, that is if Caroline and I are so fortunate as to have children some day."

Goldie shifted in her chair. "Mr. Mayor, it's not that I'm not grateful," she said, "but I am hoping to teach my own people, to help them achieve more. I hope I'm not being disrespectful, sir. Of course I am grateful for any opportunities you offer me."

"Nonsense," said Stanton. "You can be honest with me, Goldie. But, I'd really prefer you call me Zachary. Can you do that for me?"

Goldie actually snorted. Imagine calling the mayor "Zachary."

Stanton appeared unsure whether Goldie's reaction was derisive, but she wouldn't be that blatantly disrespectful, would she? "You plan on majoring in education at South Carolina State?"

"Yes, sir."

"Well, you will be pleased to know that when I am elected, I plan to propose more funding for colored schools."

Goldie thought about this for a moment. She had no idea the mayor planned to do anything for her people.

"And it's all because of you, my dear. If half the coloreds are as bright as you, they deserve the support of our government."

"Why, why, thank you, Mayor," Goldie stammered.

"Zachary, please," the mayor insisted. "Yes, unlike some of my peers, I feel that coloreds are quite capable of learning like anyone else. Having educated, self-sustaining coloreds is a whole lot better for our society. I see that this arrangement can only last for so long."

Goldie risked speaking her opinion. "I hope you are right, sir."

"Why, if things continue to change, your people may vote for me one day for president. Do you think that's possible?"

"Anything is possible, sir."

"One day South Carolina will catch up with the rest of the country."

"I hope so," said Goldie again and wondering why the mayor was up on a podium giving a speech to one little ol' colored girl.

"Tell me something, then, Goldie. What do your people need the government to do?"

It must be a set-up, thought Goldie. White men don't talk like this to girls like her.

"You can tell me, Goldie. I promise I'll listen."

There was so much Goldie wanted to say. But if she said too much, slipped up, she might reveal something about the NCRO's plans.

"I understand your hesitation. You're wondering why I'm talking to you like this."

Goldie stared at him. It was as if he could read her mind.

"You have to remember. I am not a native southerner. My ideas do not always mesh well with the locals, though I fit in where I can. I need to get what I need to get things done. I know you can understand that."

"Yes, sir." Goldie nodded reluctantly.

"That's why I'd like you to think about my proposal, Goldie."

Proposal?

"I'm not offering you just any job, but the ear of a United States senator. Just think how you could help your people's cause. I did not know your father, but from what I understand about his work, you would make him proud by coming to work for me once I am elected."

Immediately the lull Goldie had fallen into dissipated. Why was he bringing up her father? She kept her eyes lowered.

"We could be a formidable team, Goldie."

Team? Goldie couldn't believe her ears, which were now burning.

"I'll tell you something else, too. If times were different, I might think about taking you to Washington not as my secretary, but as my wife."

Goldie struggled to conceal her shock. If her legs hadn't been rooted to the floor she would have fled out the door and down the drive past the magnolias and far away from Manhattan forever. Was he crazy? What was the man looking for?

"Alas, we both know that our relationship would never be accepted," the mayor went on sadly. "It saddens me that you, such a lovely young woman, so smart and talented, have to clean my home to save for college. That's why I try to help you by adding a little extra into your paycheck, you know."

Goldie had chosen to believe that the "extra" was for all the extra hours she put in when Mrs. Stanton was on the warpath, but now she knew different.

"You have simply had the misfortune of being born during this day and age, and with that color," said the mayor. He stood and came around his desk to stand next to Goldie, whose whole body now felt numb.

"I wish I could show you off on my arm at every social gathering. I would make sure you had the best designer dresses money could buy."

Goldie had never noticed the mayor's enormous hazel eyes before. She was transfixed by them. It was as if he knew her deep inside, in her soul.

"I know what I'm asking you to do is beneath a young lady of your standards," said the mayor. "But join me in Washington on my terms and there is no telling what we could do for coloreds...as well as what we could do for each other." Here the mayor stopped and meaningfully gazed into Goldie's eyes. "As long as we had an understanding. Because of course there could never be a time we could be together in public."

The mayor was so close that Goldie could see the pores of his skin. The smell of his cologne was intoxicating. Her heart pounded in her chest. Not because she was afraid, but because her body was reacting to his proximity and words of declaration.

When the mayor took Goldie's hand, she shocked herself by not pulling away.

Then he kissed her.

The deal was sealed.

. . .

Goldie came to her senses with the snap of a rubber band.

"Stop! Mr. Mayor, wait."

Stanton pulled back, affronted. He had never been rejected before.

"I have a boyfriend," Goldie said.

"Oh, I know all about him," the mayor scoffed. "That cad Jake Freeman. But I have to be honest, Goldie, when I say I'm sure you can do a lot better than a man like that."

Goldie's reaction to this statement made Stanton backtrack quickly. "I'm sure that this Freeman is a good man, of course," he said, "but look at his lifestyle, my dear. Certainly not one that you can bank on. He could go to jail at any time. But with me, you will live well the rest of your life. You'll travel. You will personally be able to make a difference for your family and your people."

Goldie was quiet.

The mayor instinctively knew he had pushed far enough for one day. "Promise me you will think about it, my dear. I mean really think about it."

Goldie nodded slowly as the mayor kissed her on the forehead. Suddenly, her feet were no longer nailed to the floor. Pulling herself out of the deep chair she rushed out the study door and ran as if the Devil himself were behind her.

. . .

"Have a seat, girl." Miss Mable motioned for her to sit.

Now back on safer turf, Goldie made her way down the seven stairs to the bottom one. The help had arrived, the oldest up at the top, consistent with the hierarchy. The help's gossip session was apparently in full swing.

"Um-hm," Miss Mable was saying, "the man and his wife sure is havin' problems."

"Um-hm. She been complainin' that he done cut back on her house money," said Essie Mae with a tsk.

"Now, ain't that a damn shame," Miss Mable said. "No matter how her money get cut back, she still gone have lots mo' money than us."

There was a unanimous "um-um" and a shaking of heads.

Goldie assumed that they were talking about the Stewarts down the street. It couldn't be Mrs. Stanton, who was spending more than ever, if the dresses and shoes and hats in her closet were any indication.

"That's right," said Uncle Ed. "And the more he talks about runnin' for office, the mo' they talk about his real ma."

Office? "Real ma"? What were they talking about?

Then Goldie knew. They were talking about the mayor and his wife, not the Stewarts down the street.

"They say she was really in love with him," said Essie Mae.

Wait. Who was in love with whom?

"It's a shame how they took that gal's baby," added Miss Mable.

"And then gettin' fired like that by the missus. Poor thing." Uncle Ed's two cents proved that men gossiped just as much as women.

"Sho did." Essie Mae said as if she'd been there when it—whatever it was—had happened.

Goldie's mind spun round and round. She knew the mayor's wife had never been pregnant. They certainly weren't raising a child of their own or anyone else's.

"Does he even know?" Mary asked.

"Oh yeah, he knows," Miss Mable said. "He keep his birth certificate upstairs locked in his night stand. I seen it wi' my own eyes."

"No!" There were gasps all around.

"Sho enough did," insisted Miss Mable. "He keep the key on the top shelf in his armoire. Right there on it, it says, 'Mother: Coral Ann Jones. Father: Zachary L. Stanton.'"

Uncle Ed was openly disbelieving. "How did she get them to put a white man's name on her boy's birth certificate?"

"He wanted it. He loved that woman somethin' fierce."

Goldie's mind raced with the possibilities. Could it be true? That Zachary Stanton was really one of them?

A colored?

. . .

Goldie waited in the kitchen out of sight until she heard the mayor's car pull out of the driveway, then tore up the grand staircase and into the master bedroom suite. The key to the locked night stand was right where Miss Mable said it was. She inserted it in the lock, almost dropping it, her hand was trembling so badly. If this were true, if the mayor were actually colored, why, that would explain everything. Well, almost everything. Why Goldie felt such familiarity around him. Why he related to colored people more than most whites, even more than most northerners.

She had pulled out the paper and was holding it in her hands when Mayor Stanton emerged from the hallway.

Chapter 20

The look on Mayor Zachary Stanton's face had gone from angry to horrified to desperate to devastated in the second it took for Goldie to turn around and realize she'd been caught. The paper drifted to the floor as if she'd lost the will to hold it.

"Goldie...." he croaked.

Goldie picked up the paper, set it on the night stand, and attempted to make a dignified exit, but the mayor's arm shot out and held her to the spot.

She wouldn't leave his presence for another hour.

Thinking about it now, the mayor's story was still inconceivable to Goldie. How could a man destined to be president keep his race concealed and expect no one would find out? How could such a man profess his love for a colored woman—and intend never to share his true color, his true nature? Though he had answered all her questions, nothing made more sense now than before.

And she had listened! Listened to every word he'd said—after promising never to share any of it with anyone, especially Jake Freeman.

Mayor Stanton—for that is how she continued to think of him—explained how it was true, that he was as colored as she. That they'd sent his mother—his birth mother—away when he was born. It seemed he hadn't even learned that his biological mother was other than his father's wife until he married and overheard her talking to the family attorney, instructing him to ensure that Zachary would not be allowed to touch the family estate unless he married a white woman and "proved" he would pass it on to white children.

Of course, Caroline Stanton had eventually discovered their secret and now lived in terror that she would get pregnant or that it would somehow be revealed and ruin all their political—and social—aspirations. Seems the mayor's suggestion that they would have children was only a ruse.

Goldie had asked very few questions, but had a burning need to know what happened to Zachary Stanton's "real" mother. "What happened to her? Where is she? Do you see her?" she'd asked.

"Hold your horses, Goldie. It seems my parents could not have children, which was the reason my father gave for seeking comfort in Coral Ann's arms. When she gave birth to a white-looking son— me—he would have no part of giving me up. From what I hear, my mother fought the decision, but in those days, well, she had no choice. They told her that was how it was going to be, that she was welcome to stay on as my 'nanny,' but that was all. And she was never to speak of our relationship again.

"I saw her only once," said the mayor, "not too long ago. Our reunion was...bittersweet. She had held onto so much sadness...and I had to tell her that our secret had to remain intact."

Goldie had gotten angry at the ease with which Stanton had let his mother go. He was weak, a weak man with aspirations that mattered more than family. She could think of no colored man who would not cherish the ability to provide for his family, who would agree to turn his back on his own mother out of shame.

When the mayor looked at the clock and said it was time for him to prepare for President Jameson's arrival, Goldie had left quickly, feeling sullied by the whole sordid story.

The question was, would she go against her promise and share that story with Jake Freeman?

Chapter 21

"Were there a lot of mixed people living as whites back then?"

Goldie's lips formed a tight line at her daughter's question. "There was too much at stake for that, Shelby. No, I guess most lived as black. White people looked askance at such things, as if they'd had nothing to do with the result. But there was a lot of mixing where it counted—in the bedroom—so I'd imagine there must have been a lot of secrets being kept behind closed doors."

"What did you do?" asked Shelby.

"When I got to Nate's, Isaac met me at the door. The room was filled to capacity with the festivities. Any excuse would do, but with the President coming and all, this was a legitimate one."

. . .

The bar was a tipsy maze of bodies, but Isaac's bulk led Goldie through to Jake's office easily.

As soon as the door shut, she ran to Jake and buried her head in his muscular shoulder.

Jake guided her chin up so he could look at her. "Did something happen, Goldie? If anyone hurt you, I'll—"

"No!" said Goldie, "no, it's nothing like that. It's just that... that...."

Jake waited, but suddenly Goldie had remembered her promise to Mayor Stanton, a man who also loved her, at least in his own way. If she told Jake, surely he'd go off like a cannon. On the other hand, how could she keep this information to herself?

Jake held her away to see her better. "Goldie...what aren't you telling me?"

Goldie sighed. She no more had the capacity to keep secrets from Jake than from her mother. "All right, I'll tell you. But you must promise me that you'll only listen—that you won't do something you'll regret later."

"Goldie," Jake said sternly, "you know better than to ask me to make promises I might not be able to keep."

Goldie pouted. "Well, then, I can't tell you. I won't tell you."

Jake pushed her aside, a little roughly for Goldie's taste.

"Tell me now, Goldie, before I have to find out for myself. And you know I will."

Goldie looked at the man she adored. He was right. Jake Freeman had eyes and ears everywhere. Why, if Goldie remembered correctly, he was related to Miss Mable. Somehow he would find out and then there would be real trouble.

"I haven't said anything before because I didn't want you to think anything of it," she started. Immediately Jake's eyes drew together in suspicion. "But the mayor has been giving me extra time off and a bit of extra pay."

"Don't tell me that you and he—! Goldie, how could he—? how could you—? I'm gonna kill that sonova—"

Goldie grabbed Jake's arm. "No, Jake, no! It's not like that! You have to believe me. He just treats me a little special, that's all." She rushed on. "Anyway, this afternoon I was out on the porch with the rest of the help, on our break, and they were talking about the Stantons. Miss Mable said right out loud that the mayor's real mamma—that his real mamma was a colored woman."

Jake almost laughed the idea was so ludicrous. "That's crazy," he insisted. "Even if Miss Mable said it." Miss Mable, however, was rarely misinformed. She might be a terrible gossip, but her gossip generally tended toward the veracity of the word of God.

"But I'm telling you it is true, Jake. I asked him about it." Again, Goldie realized her mistake too late. What would Jake think of her conversing with the mayor?

"Oh, I see," said Jake with a sneer. "You asked him. So, seeing as he's such a nice man, he agreed to tell you everything."

Goldie lowered her eyes, then decided to tell Jake straight. She was her mamma's daughter, after all.

"No, you're right, Jake. Mr. Stanton seems to have…feelings…for me. Of course I have none for him!" she hastened to add. "None at all. And I have kept a distance between the two of us. There has never been any semblance of impropriety."

"How is that possible?" Jake said, sitting back away from her. "Surely, a white man—a colored man passing for white—with that kind of power can apply any kind of pressure he wants."

Goldie shook her head. "No. It wasn't like that, Jake. It was sad, really. I think he's lived with this secret a long time and feels bad about it. His wife is scared to death someone will find out, and he's all out there suggesting more support for issues related to us."

"Man, I can't believe it," said Jake. "You know the kind of company he keeps—including that of the sheriff and his WWO cohorts."

"I sure was angry about that, too," said Goldie. "His poor mother was sent away when he was a baby and now, even though he knows about her, he keeps her hidden away. It's a terrible thing, Jake."

167

Jake, whose own relationship with his mamma was solid as the ground he stood on, understood.

"But even if I were a free woman, I would never get together with the likes of someone who's ashamed of his own people!" Goldie said with vehemence.

At that moment Isaac knocked on the door. Jake's presence was required. Goldie told him to go on. She had to get on home.

"Just one more thing before you go, then, Goldie, and I'm serious about this. You tell your mother I don't want you working for the mayor anymore. I'm done bein' understanding. And I will personally pay for your education."

Goldie smiled graciously, took Isaac's arm, as if her mamma wouldn't balk at such a mortifying suggestion.

Chapter 22

The National Civil Rights Organization had arrived in Aiken and its members had been assigned to various homes for the duration. The fact that Mr. Winthrop Pennington was staying in the home of a widow was definitely raising some eyebrows.

Lillian Jackson was oblivious to the chatter. It was her house and she was perfectly capable of inviting anyone she chose to be her guest. On the day of his arrival, she picked the white man up at the station in the car she was so proud of. An automobile provided independence and freedom, the two things Lillian desired most.

"Were you always this independent, Mrs. Jackson, or has this come about out of necessity?"

They both knew what he meant. "I've been like this all my life," said Lillian. "And I was lucky enough to have found someone who understood me and supported me as much as I supported him."

"He must have been a special man to have someone like you speak so highly of him," said Mr. Pennington.

There was a moment of silence, but a comfortable one. A respectful one.

Winthrop Pennington was not surprised at Lillian's immaculate yet comfortable home. She led him to a small room off the kitchen with a twin-sized bed in it and then left him to freshen up. "I'll just put the kettle on for some tea," she said.

Soon they were seated at the table drinking tea and eating fresh-baked cookies.

"So, tell me about your girls, Mrs. Jackson. You are obviously an amazing role model and teacher. Do your daughters take after you?"

Lillian flushed at the compliment. "I've always hoped they'd be college bound," she said, "but they have minds of their own, so we'll have to see."

"Tell me this, then. When you were a little girl, what did you want to grow up to be?"

Caught off guard, Lillian gave the question the attention it deserved.

"Well, to be honest, I wanted to be a lawyer."

"You know, I can't say that surprises me," said Winthrop. "How did that come about?"

Lillian told him about the kind man who'd given her books to read every time he saw her as a young girl. "He was a lawyer. I loved hearing him talk about his cases, about the Constitution. It was his passion."

"If you had been born in a different time, Miss Lillian," Winthrop said gently, "I'm sure you would've made a great lawyer."

Lillian sat up straighter. "Denver and I did all right for ourselves," she said, "maybe too well for our own good. You know they don't like us to get too successful. One way or another they find a way to take it away from you."

There was a commotion on the porch saving Pennington the need to form a response. After all, he was one of "them."

"There are my daughters. I'm sure you remember them from church."

"How could I forget? They have inherited your beauty."

Lillian flushed and ignored this declaration.

"Mamma, where are you? I need to talk to you."

"Girls? We're in the kitchen. You remember Mr. Pennington from our church meeting."

Goldie and Jake slowly made their way to the kitchen.

When Lillian saw who was with her daughter, her face turned to stone.

"Goldie. What is the meaning of this? Mr. Freeman has no business in this home."

Pennington excused himself and headed for his room.

Goldie saw the expression on Jake's face and quickly filled him in on the housing situation. He decided to jump right in.

"Miss Jackson, I know you don't like me much, but I hope that what I am about to tell you will prove to you how much I love your daughter, and that I will do anything to protect her."

"I don't doubt that you love her, Jake," Lillian said calmly. "I never have. But I am her mother and where you go, mess follows. If that weren't the case, she wouldn't need protectin'."

Jake bristled, but couldn't deny the truth in the statement.

"I understand," he said solemnly. "But I love her. Which is why I have placed protection around your home."

"And I thank you for that, Mr. Freeman, but I don't need reminding. Now, is there something else you've come to say? If so, spit it out."

If there had been any question before, Jake certainly knew now how Goldie came by her outspokenness.

He stopped beating around the bush and made clear his offer to pay for the girls' education.

"Again, I thank you, Mr. Freeman. But the girls are earning money to pay for their educations."

"I don't want Goldie working for that rat mayor anymore," said Jake in a rush. "Not after what I learned tonight!"

Well, that about settled it.

Mayor Stanton's secret was about to be freed.

. . .

It was agreed. Goldie would go back to work, but this time for the Addingtons.

Jake would have preferred she go straight to college, but Mrs. Jackson would have none of it. He'd never met a prouder woman.

"Please, Mrs. Jackson, think about it," he pleaded one final time before he left. "Your husband did a lot for our people, took from his own pocket to do it, too. It's time to let others do the same for you...and your girls."

Lillian was stopped in her tracks.

"And in this case, I'll simply be helping my future wife—" Lillian and Goldie gasped "—if she'll have me," he said. "And to assure you of my integrity, if Prohibition is not repealed within the next two years, I will shut down the club or hand it over to my partner and go to work for my father."

Suddenly there was a banging on the door. Someone was yelling what sounded like, "Take cover, take cover!"

It was the neighbor from next door, Eddy Bacon, sticking his head around the screen door. "Take cover!" he repeated. He was breathing heavily and sweat poured down his forehead. "It's the Order. They're riding down Easy Street headed for the north side!"

Silently, Jake, Goldie, and Rose, who had come in the back door as they'd been talking, along with Mr. Pennington, watched from the porch as the WWO moved down the street in front of the house in full regalia, with one exception. This time some of them had been brazen enough to leave their hoods at home.

Surprising his guests, Winthrop Pennington chose to stand his ground. He might be white, but he'd never been prouder to stand side by side with anyone he'd ever known.

. . .

As Zach drove down Park Avenue to the accompaniment of the train whistle, he took in the size of the crowd. So many people had turned out to catch a glimpse of the President on his way through from the train station. Just about every citizen of the city of Aiken was milling about Park Avenue all the way to the Wilbridge Inn to catch a glimpse of the President. The mayor parked his Model A and stepped out. Wouldn't hurt to let the press know he was willing to walk amongst the people, that the mayor of Aiken led a first-class modern city ready for the future and change. He scanned the crowd for Goldie, hoping she'd be there to support him, but no familiar face stood out.

A strong young man exited the train along with five others, all dressed in similar blue suits and all scouring the bodies pressed as close as they could get to the train for possible assassins. Since the murder of another president years before, a permanent presidential detail had been approved by Congress in 1913 to protect the current president. In this case, President Jameson's liberal platform also made him a target.

The first young man held up a bullhorn. "May I have your attention, please?"

The crowd quieted, but excited murmuring continued.

"I present to you...the President of the United States."

The crowd erupted in cheers as two more Secret Service agents exited the train, followed by President Jameson and his wife and, behind them, two more Secret Service agents. The President smiled and waved, as did Mrs. Jameson. Known for her fashion sense and beauty, the First Lady was always a sight to behold, although her outspoken ways had garnered more than a couple of death threats, causing authorization for even more Secret Service agents to be deposed to her family's side.

The President held up his arms. "Please. Please. You're too kind. Please."

By now Zach had made his way to the front of the crowd where he quickly located Sheriffs Baker and Moody. The two sheriffs stood a stiff distance apart, speaking volumes about Bull's apparent antagonism.

"Good afternoon, Governor Lee, Senators, Congressmen, Mayor Stanton, and good citizens of Aiken, South Carolina. I am touched by this warm welcome to your fair city. I look forward to the many fond memories I am sure my wife and I will experience while here."

Mrs. Jameson gave a gracious smile and waved to the crowd, first to her right, then to her left.

"I would also like to thank Mayor Stanton for all his meticulous planning to make such an event possible."

Zach rocked on his heels with satisfaction. The President of the United States had personally thanked him. Him. Zachary Stanton. He was on his way, now. His dream was coming to fruition.

Amid more cheering, President Jameson stepped down and approached the mayor. "Mayor."

Zach couldn't help himself. He bowed slightly at the waist and took the President's outstretched hand. "Mr. President. It is indeed an honor. If you're ready, Sheriffs Moody and Baker here will escort you to your lodgings."

"Mr. President," someone called out from the crowd, "do you intend to address any of the social issues plaguing the south in your speech tomorrow?"

The President barely flinched, but Zach was crushed. Some idiot had had the nerve to question the President not a moment after he'd alighted from the train. The mayor waited, unsure what action he should take.

Bull's head whipped around to see which big mouth was nervy enough to barrage the President with questions. For that was what he was doing, one question tripping over the next like the clickety-clack of keys of a typewriter.

Coming from a white man. The same white man who'd been standing outside Lillian Jackson's house a short time earlier. It was some time before the President and the First Lady made their way to the Blue Landing.

. . .

Senator Jantzen from New York and his wife were the first to arrive at the Blue Landing Club. Then Senator Montreaux from Michigan. Introductions were made. Zach steered them in the direction of the ballroom, where drinks were being served. Governor Lee came next, and Zach scurried over to him to give him the proper welcome he deserved.

"Governor Lee, I was about to send a search party out for you."

The governor rolled his eyes. "You know how it is, Mayor. The missus was having a little wardrobe snafu."

Mrs. Lee rolled her eyes back at him. "Me?" she said. "Who lost his shoe and had to get three boys to look for it?"

"Well," said Zach nervously, "you both look smashing."

Five of the men from the train station entered the room and spread out, announcing the President's imminent arrival.

Zach rang the bell by the door and waited for quiet.

"Ladies and gentlemen, I present to you the President of the United States."

The applause was enthusiastic but subdued, as befitted the elite present.

Tommy Stevens was the lucky server chosen to serve the President. He was sure not to stand too close for fear of arousing the paranoia of the Secret Service. "May I offer you a drink, Mr. President?"

"Let's see, what do we have here?" said the President of the United States.

"Fine wine for the First Lady, sir, and your choice of sherry, bourbon, or cognac."

"Hmm, well, I don't know. You're not hiding any members of the press in here, are you, Mayor?" The President chuckled, but everyone knew he was serious. He could not afford to be photographed violating Prohibition, even if the law was up for repeal.

Zach stepped forward—but not too far. "I assure you, sir. There will be no press here tonight."

President Jameson helped himself to a sherry.

Zach hoped he was right.

. . .

The tables upstairs had all been arranged to form one huge U at the mayor's behest. Tonight, however, Zach would give his seat at the head of the U to the President.

Dinner was uneventful, with pleasant talk of the southern climate, local golfing, and, of course, horses. Zachary chose to avoid mention of politics altogether. He and the President both knew they would have more than one discussion that weekend about Zach's upcoming senatorial race, but tonight was not the time.

After dinner, the guests proceeded to the ballroom where the band was playing Glenn Miller's "Moonlight Serenade."

Caroline Stanton was making the rounds with the First Lady. "Ladies, I would like to introduce you to our First Lady, Mrs. Claire Jameson."

They made their way around the group of over-dressed women until they got to Caroline's sister Julia.

"And this is my sister Julia," said Caroline.

"My pleasure," said Mrs. Jameson.

"Oh no, the pleasure is all m-mine," Julia said, stuttering for the first time in her life.

"Julia's husband owns the Aiken Gazette," said Caroline, seeing her sister's social graces had momentarily left her.

Julia recovered. "If I'm not being too forward, Mrs. Jameson, I would love to do a small interview for the paper." Julia's journalism experience was negligible, but her husband owned the paper, which gave her the right to be their star reporter if she wanted to be. And she did.

Claire Jameson never shied away from an opportunity to spread the word as long as it were appropriately disseminated. "I would be glad to make a statement, Julia. The Women's Suffrage Movement could certainly use your support. If you'd be so gracious as to sign our membership roster and keeping our cause alive in your paper, that is? Why, you ladies could plan similar events throughout South Carolina."

The conversation came to a halt and went downhill from there.

Chapter 23

Zachary had led the President and Senators Jantzen, Montreaux, and Moseley into his study. Tommy had already come and gone, having poured brandies all around. This was the bigwigs' opportunity to take the pulse of the man the President appeared to support.

Senator Moseley didn't pull any punches. A hard-line teetotaler from New Hampshire, the Senator professed being flummoxed by how Prohibition could split a nation in two. Nonetheless, he had continued to vote with the National Federal Party. "If I understand correctly, President Jameson is not the first president to grace the Blue Landing Club with his presence. How is it you've managed to do so well, considering these dry times?"

Zach sat forward, in familiar territory. "The Blue Landing Club is much more than a watering hole, Senator, as you can now attest to. We have always focused on our tradition of exquisite service and food. I am confident that even were the Blue Landing Club to discontinue certain of its...offerings...our doors would remain open."

"I admit the Blue Landing Club has a fine reputation," said the Senator, apparently pacified, "as does the Wilbridge Inn."

Senator Montreaux, a golfer and horseman, nodded. Aiken appeared to be a fine vacation spot for him and his family. His frankness, however, was also legendary.

"I understand that tradition and excellent service go a long way, but I'm curious as to how you have continued to provide liquor— and some of the best liquor, I might add—and spirits when most everyone else has to make due with watered-down concoctions. After all, this is Whiskey Road!" The Senator sat back, clipped off the end his cigar, and lit it.

"Actually, Zach," President Jameson said, "John has a point. We've all heard the horror stories about the crime associated with running whiskey. The party cannot afford any association with the negativity surrounding the rum trade."

Zachary sensed he was losing points and began to perspire. Before he could respond, Senator Moseley added another ten cents.

"I've heard many rumrunners get their shipments from Canada, come right down the Detroit River to the bigger cities," he said. "Why, it's been suggested they send them down in hearses! What do you have to say to that, Mr. Mayor?"

Zachary forced a smile and took a breath. But the Senator kept pushing.

"And tell, us," he gushed, "how do you keep the gangsters in check? They are a huge problem in the big cities. I can only imagine a city the size of Aiken could be overrun."

"Gentlemen, gentlemen," said Zachary, praying his panic wasn't evident. "I will address all your concerns. First of all, I am not involved in the day-to-day operations of the club. If all goes well, what involvement I do have will virtually end. And, as far as our fair city is concerned, the mob has never showed any interest in setting up shop in Aiken."

"That may be so," said Senator Montreaux, "but despite the temperance movement's claim, violence and lawlessness increased after the Eighteenth Amendment was ratified. Federal convictions are up by five hundred percent."

"Yes, it appears that the moralists of this great nation have failed." President Jameson shook his head sadly.

Moseley wasn't done, however. "Mr. Mayor, we all know that most liquor is cut to make three or four bottles from one, then distributed to gangsters throughout the country. This despicable practice has led to countless injuries and, in some cases, death. How do you—excuse me, your club—avoid such nefarious behavior and consequences?"

And so it went.

The senators drilled Zachary Stanton. Zachary Stanton squirmed.

It was a very long night.

PART 3

Chapter 24

Winthrop Pennington's family was instrumental during the Revolutionary and Civil Wars—always taking the side it felt would best serve the nation. Having said that, his presence was likely making many of the politicians from Washington D.C. uncomfortable, given his obvious enthusiasm for monitoring the activities of the National Federal Party. Ironically, his family had historically been card-carrying National State Party members who had freed the slaves. Supporting a National Federal Party event, therefore, may have seemed strange to some people.

Though the NSP was credited with freeing the slaves, however, its message had been a mixed bag at best: "You're free. Now run and catch up as best you can." So, when the NSP failed to enforce the laws guaranteeing equal treatment and rights, many who valued those ideals began to leave the party. The National Federal Party had seen its opportunity and set out to attract black voters, at least in the north and west. The south, for the most part, took a lot longer to catch up with the rest of the nation.

The WWO supported the National Federal Party, growing out of its hostility toward the newly freed slaves. The NFP perpetrated voting stipulations throughout the south to prevent blacks from voting. When its attempts did not succeed, the party used the Order to intimidate blacks with fear and violence, frustrating many blacks and some major financial supporters enough to look elsewhere. In response, so-called independent parties began cropping up and the NFP realized it had better change its image by introducing new candidates.

Although Winthrop had never officially left the National State Party, he felt it was in his best interest to keep abreast of what was going on in the NFP, which was attempting to lure him—and his family money and reputation—to its ranks. It wasn't difficult to take full advantage, wining and dining with the same people he'd be protesting the next morning. Tonight was a prime example.

"Winthrop Pennington, why am I not surprised to find you here?" asked Congressman Byrnes of District Three of New York, his hand outstretched.

"I aim to please," said Pennington, joining Byrnes who was standing with Congressmen Lane and Mayweather.

"I believe the State Party has a banquet somewhere on the other side of the country," Congressman Lane said, which made them all chuckle.

"That may be true," said Pennington, "but I wouldn't miss this for anything. It's not every day you get to see a leopard try to change its spots."

"Touché." Congressman Mayweather loved a man who was knowledgeable and prepared. "That's what we need; someone to keep us on our toes."

Their chortles drew in the mayors of Columbia and Augusta and introductions were made.

"Mr. Pennington here has been keeping us on our toes," Congressman Byrnes repeated, looking around for the help with the liquor. "Looks like you're the only State Party member here, Pennington."

"Sure you can hold your own against the big boys?" Mayor Grant said.

"I'll do my best," Pennington parried, bemused. This fellow must not know who he was.

"Oh, I know who you are," Mayor Grant assured him, correctly reading his expression.

"Pennington, Pennington...don't tell me you're a descendant of Wentworth Pennington," said Congressman Mayweather.

Pennington toasted him with his glass. "That's me," he said.

"Despite your political associations, it's an honor to meet you," said Mayweather. "I may disagree with your family's position on various issues, but I cannot deny their great service and dedication to this nation."

Pennington again raised his glass.

"I just hope when you write about this weekend in one of your editorials," Byrnes said, "that you mention all the programs and strides we are making toward becoming a more inclusive party."

"Well, that depends on what I see and hear tomorrow. I will, as always, be fair and objective."

"I'll take it," said Byrnes.

"How about this shindig," Mayor Grant said, swirling the liquor in his glass.

They all understood the reference. They all hoped it would not become an issue during the election.

"I heard the mayor has his hands full with that Jake Freeman. Isn't he considered the biggest rumrunner around?" asked Grant, stirring the pot.

"Can't say as I know," Pennington said noncommittally.

"I heard the mayor is having quite the time keeping Freeman under control," Mayor Black added. "Even the Order has a hands-off policy, apparently."

"Sounds like the mayor has a platform already: crime control," Pennington said drily.

"And how would you deal with the problem of a criminal element that was perhaps more powerful than you if you were in our soon-to-be Senator Stanton's shoes?" asked Byrnes.

"Good question. I'll let you know when I run for office," cracked Pennington.

"No, seriously," pressed Mayor Black. "We've all had to deal with the issue in one way or another. How would you handle it?"

"It's simple. Repeal the Eighteenth Amendment," said Winthrop.

"Don't tell me you've converted from the State Party," said Mayweather.

"No, not quite. I am man enough to admit when one of my party's policies is not what's best for the country, however."

Mayor Black nodded his agreement, as did Congressman Byrnes. "The very same people who charged themselves with protecting America's morals have contributed to its rapid demise," he said.

"Sure enough," clucked Congressman Mayweather.

"Let's see...a sharp increase in organized crime, murder, and mayhem...a novel in the making," Byrnes said, but his laugh was forced.

"Lucky for them, they have people like you in the party, Winthrop," said Grant.

Winthrop inclined his head. "Why, thank you, Mayor Grant."

. . .

"I don't think the fine citizens of Aiken, or the country for that matter, want to be told to pull themselves up by the bootstraps,"

Mrs. Jameson was saying. "Can you imagine saying such a thing to people who are hurting?"

Zachary really didn't want to talk to the First Lady about politics, but he needed her husband's support. "I agree wholeheartedly. I must add that our fair city has benefitted from the Emergency Relief Agency. Our industrial workers have suffered a great deal during this depression, something that the DeJanes administration seemed to deny even existed. When they did admit economic trouble, they left it to the rest of us to fix.

"Sadly, many of our fine citizens have left in search of better opportunities—only to find, I'm sure, that it's just as bad everywhere else," surmised Zachary.

"Has the Reconstruction Finance Corporation benefitted the banks in Aiken?" asked the First Lady. She was fully aware that the men in the room wanted no part of her discourse. In this case, fortunately, she had the upper hand.

"There aren't many banks in Aiken," said the mayor. "A blessing or a curse, depending on how you look at it. I personally saw to it that some of our most deserving colored Aikenites received monies from the Federal Home Loan Bank Act."

The President heard this last comment as he joined them. "And don't you forget to remind them of that tomorrow, Zachary, and of who made it possible."

They discussed a few more details about the next day's events and then it was time to say goodnight.

"You and Caroline hosted an elegant affair, Mayor," said the President.

Zach was left at the door wondering if that remark had any deeper meaning as the First Lady took the President's arm and off they went.

Chapter 25

Lillian was soaking in the tenor of Winthrop's voice. It was late, but she'd waited until he was back, hoping he would share details about the big do at the mayor's house.

"Lillian, you shouldn't have waited up! I know you've had a long day."

"I didn't mind," said Lillian, meaning it. She busied herself with making tea.

"Well," said Winthrop, "since you're here, there's something I'd like to say."

Lillian sat down, but could not meet this man's eyes. After a lifetime of avoiding the gaze of the white man, it was a real challenge. Then there was that telling crackle between them that she had already told herself was nothing more than nerves, circumstances being what they were. "Tell me about your evening first, Winthrop," she said.

"You'll be glad to hear that there was no mention of what we have planned. The President and congressmen stuck to topics like federal programs to help the poor. They hit on Prohibition, of course, too."

"There was no mention of the federal programs reaching us specifically?"

"Well, no, but the President did express his desire to ensure that everyone has access to economic aid, especially in the south. I believe he intends to address the topic in his speech tomorrow."

"We'll see...." Lillian said, philosophically.

"I don't blame you for being skeptical, Lillian."

"Oh, I believe he'll talk about it. It's enforcing it that I have doubts about."

There was a soft knock on the door. Startled, Lillian looked at Pennington, who moved to her side. "Who is it?" she whispered, not wanting to wake the girls.

"Danny Young," a voice whispered back.

Lillian slowly opened the door. "Danny? What are you doing here so late?"

"I saw your light on."

"Danny, this is Easy Street. You aren't supposed to be roaming on this side of town this time of night."

"I know, Miss Lillian, but...."

"Wait. Here. Come on in." Lillian peered up the street in both directions quickly before stepping aside to let Danny into the kitchen where Winthrop was still standing. "It's okay, Winthrop. This is Danny Young...a friend. Danny, this is Winthrop Pennington. He's from the National Civil Rights Organization."

The direct challenge on Lillian's face kept Danny from saying something, but his expression said what half the town was probably thinking about her choice to invite a white man into her home. He also knew Lillian Jackson didn't care one whit what other people thought. "Do you need something, Danny?" she prodded.

"I sure hate to ask, Miss Lillian, but Judi and me having a real hard time. I wouldn't ask for myself, you understand, but on a count of her and the kids, I ain't got no choice but to beg. She still got her job at the Wilbridge, but I done lost mine, and—"

"Stop, Danny. You know you don't have to beg me for anything. I'll put together a food package for you. It should carry y'all for a few days. Have you applied for aid?"

Danny nodded gloomily. "But you know they put us at the bottom of the list. Who knows when that gone come through?"

"On Monday, I want you to go by the churches and use one of their relief plans."

"But Miss Lillian, I don't go to none of them churches. They ain't gone help me."

"Danny Young, I've heard just about enough. You know that church helps everybody in Aiken, even po' whites, if they asked. Everybody's hurting right now." Lillian retrieved a box and began placing some canned goods, a few packages of meat, and a big bag of rice inside.

Danny and Winthrop had not said a word to each, but were glaring at one another as if to see who could outstare the other.

"Here you go, Danny. You tell Judi I said hey and to come see me sometime."

"Yes, ma'am. I sho' will," he said. "Thank you." He shuffled to the door.

Suddenly Winthrop spoke. "You hang in there, Mr. Young. It'll get better."

Danny's lips tightened, but he left without a word.

"I'm sorry," Lillian said to Winthrop. "He was rude and you are my guest."

"I understand," said Winthrop. "It's hard for people to change."

Lillian sat down tiredly.

"Lillian, I want to give you something."

"What would you want to give me?" she asked.

"A check."

"Winthrop!" Lillian got up, nearly spilling her cold tea. "I don't want your money. In fact, I'm insulted that you even...."

"Calm down, please, Lillian. It's not what you think." Winthrop placed his hand on her arm. "I'd like you to use it to store extra food and supplies for those in need. I see how giving you are. This way, you can still provide for your own family. You all have to live, too."

Lillian sat down again to consider, her anger gone. Taking the money was uncomfortable. On the other hand, think of how many families she might be able to help. She made up her mind. "I am a woman who lives by common sense, Mr. Pennington," she said. "This money will indeed help many of those who are in desperate situations. I will accept it, and be grateful."

. . .

For the next hour Winthrop regaled Lillian with stories from his night at the Stantons until she was too woozy from lack of sleep to hear any more. "I'm keeping you up far beyond your bedtime," he finally said, "and I can see you need your rest."

He was right. But first Lillian needed to know about the First Lady—her first love's wife.

"Well, she's extremely intelligent—but you know that already. She needs to be to keep up with the President. He's on top of every subject imaginable. And the ladies can't get enough of him," he teased.

"Oh, he's all right," Lillian said dryly. If only Winthrop knew just how attractive she found Liam Jameson.

"It appears that he genuinely wants what is best for this country, and that means making sure everyone gets access to what this great nation has to offer."

"I hope you're right, Winthrop," Lillian said. "I you're right."

"But you should have seen Zachary Stanton's face when the First Lady insisted on joining in the men's conversation. For all his forward stance, it was clear he didn't like it one bit."

"I've never really liked that man," admitted Lillian. "And I know he doesn't respect women or coloreds. That's what self-loathing will do to you, I guess."

"What do you mean?"

Immediately Lillian realized her mistake. If she weren't so tired she never would have blurted out such a statement. But now it was too late. Winthrop would surely keep after it until he wormed it out of her. And why should she keep it a secret, anyway? What was the point now?

"I know you won't believe this," she said, lowering her voice even more, "but it seems our dear soon-to-be-Senator Zachary Stanton is a lot more like us than we thought."

"'Us'?" repeated Winthrop.

"Yes, us," said Lillian. "As in colored. As in, not quite white."

"No! It can't be." Whatever Winthrop might have expected, it was not this. "Are you sure? How do you know?"

"Goldie. She's been working for him. The man is infatuated with her. She learned the truth from one of the help and he admitted it."

"Stanton has got to know that if his secret gets into the wrong hands, it could be used to manipulate him—or blackmail him. Or much, much worse," said Winthrop pensively.

"What will you do, Winthrop?"

"I don't know. I don't know what could be gained by revealing it—not by me, anyway. But either way, if I think it's something I should share, I will run it by you first."

"You don't have to consult me," said Lillian, surprised.

"Nonsense. And it'll give me one more reason to see you in the future."

"You don't need a reason," said Lillian, suddenly shy. "You may see me anytime you like."

. . .

"I like the sound of that," said Winthrop, Zachary Stanton forgotten. "I am concerned, though, dear Lillian. I wouldn't want to make things any more difficult for you than they already are."

Lillian waved her hand as if pushing the gossip aside. "Let me worry about that," she said.

"I know you're a strong woman, Lillian, but just look at that Danny fellow. He was none too happy about my sitting here. By tomorrow everyone in Aiken will know I'm staying here."

When Lillian didn't respond, Winthrop reached over and kissed her gently on the cheek. "I'm no stranger to gossip, Lillian. Sometimes it's good and sometimes it's bad. And I don't live my life according to what other people think or expect of me. And I believe you live the same way."

Lillian nodded.

"Then will you accompany me to the Presidential Ball tomorrow night?"

"What! Winthrop. That's impossible and you know it!"

"It's not impossible," insisted Winthrop. "Come with me to the ball."

"You know coloreds are not allowed to dine—or anything else 'sides clean—at the Blue Landing Club. They won't even let me through the front door. You must be far more tired than I am."

"Lillian, they are not going to turn you away, and I'll tell you why."

Lillian acknowledged he had her attention.

"First, the National Federal Party knows it is on display in front of the entire nation. Imagine the hot water if the international press were to see them turning you away—or any other colored person."

"Oh, Winthrop. You are so naïve," said Lillian." They don't care. This is their culture, their heritage, their way of life. They will protect it no matter what. They want to be seen protecting it."

But Winthrop could see that the activist side of Lillian was warming to the idea.

"To a point you may be right," Winthrop conceded, "but they are also desperate to change that image. Secondly, they not only want a sizeable donation from my family but are hoping I'll convert to the Federal Party. You know my family's reputation."

"No, I don't," said Lillian, realizing she knew nothing about Winthrop Pennington aside from his connections to organized activism.

"Trust me, Lillian. There is a lot at stake."

Lillian thought for a minute. "I still can't go, Winthrop. Even if all that's true."

"But why?"

"Because I don't have a thing to wear."

They started to giggle. Soon the two were laughing so hard they had to wipe their eyes of the tears.

Finally, Winthrop recovered enough to say, "Lillian, I know you've sewn for most of the ladies who will be at that ball tomorrow. There is no question you can whip something up for yourself, if you choose. Or, better yet, I'll buy you a dress tomorrow."

"No! I couldn't!" The mere thought had Lillian in stitches—no pun intended. A man buy her a dress? Never.

"Well," she admitted reluctantly, "I do have some leftover fabric and sequins."

"There, see?" said Winthrop. "Perfect. It's a date."

Chapter 26

Practically the whole of Aiken had gone to sleep that night with expectations about the next day, many of them great.

Not Bull Baker. He woke up out of sorts and irritable after an almost sleepless night, even though he'd been exhausted from the full day and even fuller evening. His excitement at being in the President's proximity was waning. Sheriff Moody from Columbia was wearing on his patience. Worst of all, his anger at Stanton for insisting Bull stay at the Wilbridge Inn had risen with each passing hour. Yes, it was temporary. Yes, it would pay off in the end. Why, even if Stanton didn't live up to his word with respect to rewarding Bull, Stanton would be out of the way. Bull might consider running for mayor himself.

"Mornin', Sheriff Baker. Ready for some breakfast?" Emmitt Lee, the headwaiter at the Wilbridge Inn, and the other workers always ate breakfast at the table pushed into the corner of the huge kitchen. The free meal was a good perk during the hard times of the Depression.

"Don't mind if I do," said Bull hesitantly. His discomfort aside, the cooks at the Wilbridge Inn sure could cook.

"I'm sho' it ain't nuthin' like Laney's," said Lee, "but it'll hit the spot just the same." Just as Bull went to sit down at the table, all five men who were sitting there stood up to give it over to him. There was a moment of extreme tension—at least for Bull. "Is there another table 'round here?" he asked.

"No, sir."

"Well, y'all sit down, then," Bull said gruffly. "Ain't no need to eat standing up."

"Yes, sir," they said, sneaking looks at each other before sitting back down with their plates in their hands.

Judi Young, Danny's wife, sat a plate of shrimp and grits smothered with butter and gravy, a side of bacon and ham, and hoecakes in front of Bull, along with a piping hot cup of coffee. "This sho looks good, Judi."

"Thank you, Sheriff. You know how I do."

Bull tucked in, ashamed for thinking the meal was a step above his wife's cooking.

"So, Sheriff," said Johnny Adams timidly, "what is it like being with the President?"

"Shit, he's just like any other man, puts his pants on one leg at a time just like you and me."

The men at the table laughed at the joke, but Bull wasn't quite sure if they were laughing at his joke because he was white and the sheriff or if they really thought it was funny.

"Truth be told, I gotta try and keep Laney away from the First Lady. She is nagging me to death to meet the President, too. Women...." This time the men agreed wholeheartedly and the tension lessened another notch.

Before Bull had finished his breakfast, a commotion in the lobby called for his attention. Sure enough, the Secret Service detail had arisen at the crack of dawn and the President and his wife were waiting for their first meal of the day.

They were led to the dining room by Emmitt Lee. Since the Secret Service men had eaten much earlier, the room was empty save for the President and the First Lady. The Secret Service detail was posted at every single entrance and exit.

Bull felt distinctly like a lower-class citizen. He could not afford the Wilbridge Inn's meals on his salary; in fact, his breakfast this morning had been his first meal there in all his years. He'd just settled into his official police stance when he spotted Sheriff Moody and a couple of his deputies with huge platters of food at a table behind a potted plant just inside the doors to the dining room. Bull felt a snarl rise in his throat.

"Morning, Sheriff."

Bull turned as the Stantons came through the doors. "Mayor, Mrs. Stanton."

"Everything is running smoothly, I take it. The locals aren't trying to bother the President, are they?"

"No, sir, it's all under control."

"Good. Be sure to thank Sheriff Moody for helping you out this weekend."

It'll be a cold day in hell, thought Bull, but nodded as he was expected to do.

The Stantons joined the Jamesons. The mayor was determined to get down to business.

"I'm sure Mrs. Jameson would love to see our magnificent grounds," Zachary suggested, hoping Caroline would take the hint to remove Claire from the table.

"They are lovely," the First Lady said. "I had a nice walk this morning before breakfast."

Shoot. Zachary needed a plan B, but nothing sprung to mind.

"So, are you two gentlemen ready to inspire a nation today?" the First Lady went on, providing him with an out—for the moment.

"I'm certainly going to try," said the President. "But it will be up to Zachary here to carry the ball home."

Since no one really cared what the mayor had to say, this was a gracious statement by the President. People were there to hear President Jameson. All Zachary had to do was stay on point with the message and make the President appear to be supporting the right man.

"We hope you're enjoying Aiken," said Caroline.

"We certainly are," said the President. "It appears to be a rather peaceful community compared to many other southern cities."

"That's right," Zachary said. "There's very little crime and we pride ourselves on—"

"No, what I meant was peace with the colored community," interrupted the President.

"Oh. Oh, I see," said Zachary.

"My people have done some digging," said the President, "and to our surprise we did not find too much evidence of the Order's running rampant in these parts."

"We enjoy a peaceful coexistence with the coloreds in Aiken," Caroline said a bit pompously, just as Mrs. Jameson began speaking, this time without her signature smile. She zeroed in on Zachary and Caroline like a dog on a bone.

"Of course we did hear about that unfortunate incident a while back—the Denver Jackson murder, I believe."

"Tragic," agreed the President.

"Tragic," parroted Zachary and Caroline rigidly.

The President gave Zachary a long, studied look. "As you know, Zach, the Federal Party has a long history of excluding coloreds, especially in the south. Since South Carolina is strictly an NFP state, not allowing coloreds to vote in the primary is unacceptable. Over the years, our ancestors have benefitted from slavery, and we continue to benefit years after its supposed demise. I'm looking at the future, Zachary, and I hope you'll be going along with me.

"Look," the President said before Zach could form a response, "I know I'm not too popular down here. Nonetheless, I—my wife and I, that is—plan to forge ahead and carry this party into the future even if it's kicking and screaming." The President chuckled. Zach and Caroline managed to perk up their mouths into the semblance of a smile.

"To be frank," asserted the First Lady, "we want to know if you share our vision for the National Federal Party and for the United States, Mr. Mayor."

The mayor desperately did not want to have this conversation in front of the women. Who did this woman think she was, questioning Zachary's motives for serving the public? He now understood why people disliked the First Lady so. He coughed to clear his throat of his anger before saying, "Naturally, I agree wholeheartedly. I don't want the south to be left behind the rest of the country. I have grown to love it here just as much as my birthplace up north. And as far as the Order, I remain in constant contact with their leadership to make it clear that violence will not be tolerated."

The President and his wife nodded in unison. "Good to hear, Zach, good to hear," he said. "Because I plan to use the Jackson murder to demonstrate that change is imminent and necessary."

"Yes, sir, understood, sir," said Zachary, wishing he were anywhere else. "But people down here are quite set in their ways, too, sir, if I might say so. Too much of a push to force them to give up their traditions and heritage will only be rejected outright."

"Excuse me?" The President put down his fork.

The mayor blanched. "I didn't mean to offend you, Mr. President."

"No offense taken, Zach, none taken. However, I do plan to open a federal investigation into the Jackson murder. If nothing else, we have to send a message to coloreds that the Federal Party is there for them, too. For that matter, we have to send some kind of message that America will protect them even though the anti-lynching bill was not passed."

. . .

When Bull heard President Jameson say he was authorizing a federal investigation into the Jackson murder, he gasped in utter disbelief.

"Mr. President," Stanton was saying, or more like it groveling, his heart pounding, "I will see to it that everyone knows that they are to cooperate fully with the federal investigators."

Bullshit, thought Bull.

"Good," said the President. "Because they're here and plan to start early Monday morning after all this hoopla is over. We may anger a few whites, but think of how many more coloreds we'll attract to the party." When the mayor said nothing, the President added, "I am meeting with party officials to discuss allowing them to participate in the South Carolina Federal Party primaries."

Zachary managed, "I will support the party and you in any way I can, Mr. President, I hope you know that."

Fuming, Bull watched the four at the table fake smiles all around. Clearly, the mayor would sell his good ol' buddy the sheriff down the river at the drop of a hat. Maybe while the feds were snooping around they'd stumble across a certain wannabe senator in an illegal rum deal. Since Stanton insisted on being present for the planned bust of Jake Freeman, he'd also be present when the Blue Landing Club received its shipment in front of the feds. This was one sheriff who'd show the mayor that he wasn't some dumb hick looking to take the heat for a murder no one cared about anymore.

Chapter 27

"We heard the President and the First Lady took a tour of Aiken that morning, but we never saw hide nor hair of them," said Goldie. "Of course, we were too busy working."

"You got that right," said Rose. "The only one who saw her was Mamma."

"How did she manage that?" asked Shelby.

"It was Winthrop's doing. Mamma managed to see her twice, once at the rally and once at the ball."

"You mean Grandmamma actually got to go? What happened?"

. . .

The stage was set. White linen covered the tables and chairs. The podium, upon which the President of the United States would endorse Zachary Stanton's candidacy for the United States Senate, was in place. Zachary's name was on the banners that adorned the stage. Everything was perfect.

Well, almost everything.

Goldie Jackson had not agreed to stand by his side—his metaphorical side, that is. The more Zachary thought about the risk he'd taken by sharing his feelings for her, the more concerned he became. He loved her, that much was clear. He had for a long time. But he had suffered a dire lapse in judgment in telling her the extent of his feelings. If she felt otherwise, as much as it might cause him pain, he would have to make sure his secret remained safe. It would not be pleasant, but it was exactly matters like this for which he had Sheriff Bull Baker in his pocket.

People were starting to arrive. Zachary quickly motioned for his staff to assist guests to their seats. The lawn at the Blue Landing Club was covered with about one hundred white wooden chairs. The front two rows were reserved for important guests, the rest for the old money of Aiken. The area behind the chairs was standing room only, set aside for the rest of Aiken—white Aiken. The section to the right of the stage was reserved for the press. The radio stations and newspaper columnists were already in place. Zachary dashed inside the Blue Landing Club to look over his speech one more time.

He'd just taken his notes out of his suit jacket when one of his staff informed him that the President had arrived. He was thirty minutes early.

Zachary stuffed his notes back into his pocket and scurried downstairs to meet the President, First Lady, and the rest of their entourage. He barked orders along the way.

"Please forgive me for not greeting you as you arrived, Mr. President," Zach gushed. He was relieved to see that Caroline was with them.

They walked onto Stanton Field, where Zach and Caroline took their seats. President and Mrs. Jameson stepped onto the stage. The President's aide was already at the podium. He approached the microphone. "Ladies and gentlemen," he said, waiting for quiet, "the President of the United States."

The President made his way to the microphone amidst a thunderous round of applause. It lasted so long he finally had to motion for the crowd to settle down. Then he began to speak.

. . .

Lillian felt the blood wash through her veins as she strolled onto the grounds of the Blue Landing Club for the first time as a "guest," not the help. The lawn was immaculate and beautiful, with flowering trees framing the field where people were gathering for the day's events. The landscaping made her think of Denver and a tear came to her eye. This time, however, she was surprised to see that the anger had been repaced by a certain peace instead.

Lillian stepped alongside Winthrop Pennington, leading other members of the National Civil Rights Organization and a number of black Aikenites. They all carried signs with slogans like, "Equality Now," "Equal Protection Under the Law," "One Man One Vote," and "Outlaw Lynching."

One of the Secret Service agents was in their path in a flash. "You all are going to have to leave. Right now. This is a private rally."

"We are the National Civil Rights Organization," Winthrop said loudly, "and we have a right to be here."

Zachary tore off the stage, mortified at what he heard, the words flying through the air for all to witness. As he neared the confrontation, he spotted the sheriff and gave him a look to kill. Bull, not one to mince words, drew his gun and instructed the deputies to spread out across the protesters to prevent them from moving forward.

"What's going on here?" Zachary demanded.

"We've got it under control," said the Secret Service agent.

"Clearly, you do not have it under control, or these...interlopers would not be on private property," said Zach, fairly spitting with ire.

"We have some issues that we believe our President should acknowledge," Winthrop spoke up again loudly. "We have the right to be present and hear him address them."

The Secret Service agent looked from Winthrop to the mayor to the sheriff, unsure of his next move. The President's safety was his first concern, and one gun had already been pulled.

"I should've known you'd try something like this," snarled Zach. He turned to Bull. "Get these people out of here right now. The President is waiting."

"Mr. Mayor?" It was President Jameson, no longer on the podium where he belonged, but at Zachary's side.

"Sir, you really must get back on the stage," one of the Secret Service agents said.

"I agree, sir," concurred Zachary. "We have this all under control."

"Maybe so, but that doesn't answer my question." The President stepped forward. "Why, it's Winthrop Pennington. I might have guessed."

"Mr. President."

Lillian could do nothing but gape.

Then the President saw who was standing next to Pennington. It couldn't be! Impossible! But it was. Elle! The girl he'd loved. The girl he'd never forgotten.

Somehow Liam Jameson managed to regain focus. "Gentlemen. Obviously, this is a peaceful rally. Let these people in."

It was Zach's turn to gape. "But, sir, I really don't think—"

"Lesson number one, Zach. Never turn away potential voters." The President could not trust himself to look in Elle's direction again.

Zachary was aware that such "voters" were no good to him as they weren't allowed to vote in the primaries. What was the President up to? With no answer forthcoming, he had no choice. He and the Secret Service agent waved in Winthrop, Lillian, and the rest of their group.

The President turned to leave, saying, "You all can put away your signs. I plan to allay all your concerns in just a few moments. Please enjoy the speeches." By then, however, the press had snapped photo after photo: the President opposite the mayor; opposite Winthrop Pennington and the NCRO. Careers would be made on the backs of some of them.

Then the President turned back. "On second thought...I would dearly like to hear from one of these activists, Mr. Mayor." He looked at Lillian. "I'd be most grateful, ma'am, if you would be so kind as to share with me what brought you out here today—what would cause you to take such a risk."

Before Lillian took a breath to answer, the President went on, "Stanton, is there somewhere I can speak with Miss...?"

"Mrs.," whispered Lillian, "Mrs. Jackson."

Zachary kept a small office near the kitchen. He pointed wordlessly in that direction.

The Secret Service unhappily trailed the President and his companion in silent confusion. A couple of them ran ahead to check out Zachary's office.

. . .

Finally, the President and Lillian were alone. The door and all the shutters were closed.

"Elle," he said.

"Liam," said Lillian, his name a sigh.

They were in each other's arms before they had a chance to consider the ramifications.

209

"What are we going to do?" said the President. "Now that I've found you—how I've yearned!—how can I ever let you go again?"

Lillian's tears flowed. "You're not thinking straight, Liam— Mr. President. Don't forget who you are. Who I am. It is impossible, just as it was so many years ago."

"But you're not married...are you, Lillian?"

"Not anymore," said Lillian deflecting the question, "but you are!"

The President knew in that moment that the fantasy he had stoked since he'd last seen Lillian would never be realized. His shoulders slumped in defeat.

After one more long embrace, a few more words, and a moment to collect themselves, Liam opened the door to the Secret Service and escorted Lillian to the front of the crowd, which was restless and already speculating on the President's untoward behavior. The whites in the vicinity stepped back surreptitiously, hoping the President would not notice. Then the President waved to Winthrop to join Lillian.

"We will deal with this matter later," the mayor hissed to the sheriff.

. . .

President Jameson cleared his throat for the second time and began to speak. The crowd took a moment or two to settle down, but soon was rapt with interest in the President's words.

"I would like to thank you for coming out today to support me, our country, and Mayor Stanton as well. It is a testament to his accomplishments in the fine city of Aiken. Secondly, I would like to thank the fine citizens of Aiken for allowing my entourage and other distinguished guests to besiege your city. Lastly, I would like to thank you for being so gracious as we corrected our error of overlooking some of Aiken's other important citizens." President Jameson extended a glance to Lillian and then a more far-reaching one all the way to the Aikenites relegated to the very rear of the field. Although there was a slight shuffling of feet, no other reaction could be seen or heard.

"We all are aware of the difficult times facing our country," said the President. "The unemployment rate has soared to unimaginable heights. As you may well remember, during my election bid, the debate was largely over the causes and possible remedies of this Depression. We now know that the hard times we face as a nation are a result of failing National State Party policies during the last administration's tenure. To make matters worse, they continuously told you that the economy was sound or that it was bouncing back. You were told to ride it out and 'pull yourselves up.' Unfortunately, it's not that simple.

"But I am not here to talk about the failed policies of the State Party. I am here today to answer your call. You elected me decisively. I believe that gives me the mandate I need to take this country forward with bold economic and political remedies. I plan to continue to use the federal government's authority to heal our nation. I refuse to wait until the rest of the world recovers.

"Instead, we need new policies to propel this country back into a leadership position in the economic world.

"To accomplish this feat, I propose strict regulations whenever a security is sold on the stock exchange. Members of the National Federal Party and I have worked diligently to develop the National Insurance Corporation for Deposits. This program will ensure that no hardworking American loses his or her money to a bank that fails. Now, all banks will insure deposits up to $50,000."

The crowd applauded and hooted enthusiastically in support of the President's new program. "The National Insurance Corporation for Deposits will be up and running by January of next year," he continued. "And I can see by your response that you are on board with our program. That's good. But there is one good thing that has come out of these hard economic times. The American people have found a renewed interest in their government and how it is run. While some of my colleagues may not appreciate the criticism and scrutiny, I very much appreciate your interest. These hard times have certainly proven that rich or poor, we all have a stake in how our government functions and is managed.

"Millions of Americans are out of work. When I accepted the office of the presidency, I pledged to turn around the unemployment rate and as a result established the Civilian Forestry Corps to construct camps in various areas across the country. This program provides employment to desperate young men and simultaneously replenishes the soil and trees. I know the citizens of Aiken value our natural resources." The President waved his arm. "Your beautiful city is a testament to that."

This time the crowd roared and rose to its feet.

When they settled, the President went on to describe his proposal for the Agriculture Renewal Act, backed by a tax on industries that process crops, and the National Industrial Act, which would set regulations for fair business practices.

He then spoke about Prohibition. "As we continue to move away from the DeJanes' Administration failed policies, we also take an unprecedented step to repeal the Eighteenth Amendment of the Constitution. You all know the repeal was proposed in the United States Congress on February 20 of this year. I expect it will be ratified by December of this year. I know those responsible for the temperance movement had good intentions, but Prohibition has proved to be yet another failure for this country. One only has to look at the transfer of the Prohibition Bureau from the Treasury Department to the Department of Justice for proof. I fully expect to remove the Alcohol Beverage Unit from the Department of Justice.

"And now, something that must be addressed before another day passes. We must ensure some of our most valued citizens that they will not be forgotten."

The crowd knew what was coming. Their silence said it all.

The President gaze fell directly on Lillian Jackson and Winthrop Pennington. "I know you all were prepared to protest today, and I must say I appreciate your willingness to listen to what I have to say first. I have received reports of your being sent to the back of the bread lines for leftovers. I know that some of you have been turned away completely. I am here to say to you: This is not fair!

"My administration will begin to enforce laws that are already on the books. Even though the anti-lynching law was not passed in Congress, I have brought federal agents with me from the Bureau of Investigation." There was a collective gasp as the crowd took in the President's words. "These agents are here to open an investigation into the recent death—or, I should say, murder—of Denver Jackson!"

. . .

After the President dropped his bombshell, the crowd could not be hushed. Jameson continued his speech, including his ringing endorsement of "Zachary Stanton for Senator," but not many heard anything after the President had spoken the name of Denver Jackson and put it in the context of murder.

Zach felt each step to the podium as if it were his last. Instead of the good will he'd expected, there were rumblings and hushed conversation following the President's "announcement." Zach gave his speech, but with none of the zeal he'd intended. Then it was time to wrap it up.

"If the good people of the State of South Carolina choose me to represent you in Washington, I pledge to make sure that our young men have access to the Civilian Forestry Corps. I pledge to ensure that those left behind have a working, viable Civil Corps to participate in near their communities. I pledge to aid the farmers who provide not only food but jobs for others in the community, and I will support fair business practices for...."

Zachary trailed off. A face in the crowd had caught his attention. It couldn't be! But, yet, it looked just like her, at least how he remembered her. His mother?!

He did a double-take, but the woman was gone. He must be going crazy from all the stress.

The President cleared his throat, bringing Zach back from his momentary—he hoped—dementia.

"...business practices for all," Zach finished lamely.

Lillian poked Winthrop in the ribs. "Wonder what's wrong with him."

"He probably thought he saw a ghost," chuckled Winthrop, earning him a suspicious look from the woman at his side.

. . .

At long last, the speeches and fanfare were over. "I want to speak to you. Now. In my office," Zach told Bull. They made the short journey silently, the mayor's step clipped.

Once there, Zach exploded. "What in the hell was that? We had an understanding. You're being paid to keep those people quiet."

"This was not my doing," said the sheriff. "You want me to tell you what happened? Fine. I'll tell ya'. My boys prolly got wind of this federal investigation that's 'bout to go down. They ain't willin' to risk you sending yo' feds after them for tryin' to do what you tol' 'em to do."

"That's bullshit and you know it!" Zachary yelled. "All that federal investigation talk was just bullshit to win over the nigger vote. They'll come down here for a bit, get bored, and leave with nothin'. Because nobody is going to cooperate." Then the mayor turned, his voice placating. "Besides, you know I wouldn't let the feds get near you on those charges. You're my right hand man."

Bull said nothing. Though the mayor flip-flopped worse than a fish on a hook, he'd never ever heard him use the "n" word before.

"Plus, I trust you'll find a way to steer them in another direction."

"And what about your precious Goldie Jackson and her family? You think they ain't gone be pleased to send them our way?"

"Our way? What do you mean our way? I didn't have anything to do with that. In fact, I've told you time and time again to leave that goddamn Order alone."

"I do recall somethin' of the sort comin' out your mouth," said the sheriff, "but you're in this as deep as I am."

"You can't prove anything!" The mayor was back to yelling. "You fuck with me, Bull Baker, and I swear I will hang your ass out to dry so fast you won't know what hit you!"

"I don't have to prove a damn thing," Bull said calmly. "All I have to do is make the allegation."

Zachary threw his head back and took a deep breath to gather his wits.

"Now, see here, Bull, we've both been under a lot of stress these last days. Let's not get all bent out of shape. I'll tell you what. Come by my office on Monday, and we'll work something out. Hell, we can even blame it on some rogue group from another county."

Bull nodded slowly, but knew Zachary would sell him out as sure as the Order was white.

Chapter 28

Rose and Goldie Jackson had strict orders from their mother not to stray from their home on the day of the President's speech, yet the temptation was far too enticing. To see the President and the First Lady would be life-altering, of course, but to see their mother making history? Why, there was nothing that could keep them away. At the moment they were hidden behind a big rhododendron with huge red blooms, giggling like the schoolchildren they were.

They got there just as President Jameson was leading Lillian to the front of the crowd. "What's she doing up there?" Goldie whispered to her sister, pointing. Rose shrugged, starry-eyed at all the finery.

"Um-hm. That's her and him. Lillian Jackson and Winthrop Pennington." Charlene Blackmon, a notorious gossip, was standing right in front of them, speaking up so the whole world could hear. "You know, that civil rights leader who spoke at church."

"Bold as can be," agreed Vickie Stone. "And I hear tell he stayin' at Lillian's house. Imagine! A white man!"

"And they say," Charlene looked around to see if anyone were in radius of her resonant voice, "there's somethin' goin' on between the two. You know his sister never came with him."

"Hush yo' mouth," Vickie Stone said, drooling at the delicious gossip. "How do you know?"

"Danny Young. He was there just last night. Can you imagine? Lillian Jackson foolin' 'round with a white man, um-hm, and after what they did to poor Denver."

Goldie cleared her throat loudly. The women looked around, seeing no one until Goldie poked her head up out of the rhododendrons. When the women recognized the Jackson girls, they were stricken with embarrassment. Not that it took the smirks off their faces! If the sisters hadn't been in such a precarious position of their own, they might have given the gossips a piece of their mind, even if they were church ladies a lot older than themselves. As it was, glaring silence was the best they could do.

. . .

The mayor's strange behavior during his speech had Bull wondering. Stanton had always appeared cool and collected, even under duress. What could have set him off like that? As far as Bull could tell, the mayor had been going along fine until he'd looked into the crowd and gone pale as a sheet. As if he'd seen a ghost.

Bull was still pondering the events of the day when he sat down for dinner with Laney.

"You haven't said a word," she said, pouting.

Sometimes, with no one else to confide in, Bull succumbed to sharing his thoughts with his wife. He surely couldn't talk to anyone in the Order; their resentment of Stanton's limitations on their activities made their opinions far too biased to be of any use.

"It's that damn Stanton, that's all."

"The mayor? What did he do now?"

"What do you mean, 'now'?"

"Bull, I'm no fool. I know you're stuck between a rock and a hard place, tryin' to please him and the locals. Aiken is a small town. You know how people talk."

Bull sighed. "I been goin' the extra mile for the mayor all this time. It sho' won't hurt to have somebody like that lookin' out for me when he gets to be senator."

"So, what's the problem?"

"I'll tell you what the problem is. Zachary Stanton is one selfish man. He's been on my ass to keep the Order under control—you know, keep 'em off the coloreds' asses. I been doin' my best."

"Lemme guess. Then Denver Jackson got killed."

Bull nodded. "Honestly, Laney. That one was personal. I didn't want Jackson to die. I know he was a colored, but he was okay. I mean, he always kept his word and shit. I told the boys to beat his ass a bit, not kill him. You know. Send a message to other coloreds to leave white women alone. But no. Jackson promised he'd take his beatin' like a man, but then he had to go and fight back. It's a damn shame, that's what it is."

Laney got up to put the last piece of chicken she was frying on the platter. Sometimes it was best to keep her opinions to herself.

"Ever since then, it's been 'the President this' and 'the President that.' If I hear one more thing about Stanton's damn 'image' I won't be accountable for my actions." Bull's food was cooling off rapidly, but he didn't notice. "He's been promising me—and you, Laney—promising us the world if I stuck with him. But now—"

Laney slapped the spatula down on the counter. "Now you listen here, Sheriff Bull Baker, and you listen good. Don't you apologize for nothin'. Those uppity northerners come down here and enjoy our beautiful town because of people just like us, and they ain't got no right to judge. We were doing just fine before Zachary Stanton showed up. We'll do just fine when he takes his ass to Washington, too."

Bull sat back, stunned.

"You're a smart man, Bull. You provide for your family, and we ain't wanting for nothin'."

"Yeah, I'm smart, all right. Who do you think told the Order to let them troublemakers onto Whiskey Road?" Bull said with bluster. "You shoulda seen the look on his face. Nope, I ain't done with him yet."

The sheriff's words were brazen, but fell flat in the hot room smelling of fried grease.

. . .

"Who would've guessed that you're such a big mukety-muck?" said Winthrop.

Lillian, still reeling from her reunion with Liam, had no answer for that.

"I can't believe our luck! Imagine. The President choosing you, asking for your opinion. Tell me everything! What did you talk about? What did he say? This will be better than any press we could have hoped for."

"Slow down, Winthrop, please," said Lillian. "I need to think."

To meet Liam again, to hear that he still had feelings for her, it was too much for her brain—and her heart—to take in all at once. It had left her weak with fatigue. Winthrop looked at her, not comprehending her dilemma in the slightest. Instead, he believed it was simply shock at the attention she'd received by the President of the United States.

Finally, she said, "I'm just so grateful no one was hurt, what with all the ammunition...the federal police and all. I figured Bull would have men posted at Barnwell Avenue to stop those from this side of town." Winthrop hadn't known that the Jacksons were one of only a few colored families who'd ever been allowed to live on the white side of Easy Street.

"We sailed right through," Winthrop said excitedly. "Either somebody fell down on the job or they wanted Zachary Stanton to have a very difficult day."

"I know. It makes you think, doesn't it," agreed Lillian. "It was almost too easy."

"Hey, I'll take it," Winthrop said, raising his glass of water to his fellow activist.

. . .

It did not escape the attention of Goldie and Rose, who had returned home and were hunkered down as close as they could possibly be to the kitchen, that the two adults were sitting awfully close together. Goldie could also not help feeling slightly provoked by the fact that her mother was permitted to carry on this kind of illicit relationship right out in the open (so to speak) when Goldie had to stop seeing Jake Freeman!

. . .

"Now, don't keep me in suspense," said Winthrop. "What did you two talk about?"

"The President was very kind," Lillian said, attempting to stray as little as possible from the truth. "He told me we were brave and asked about the most important issues we felt needed addressing. You know, that kind of thing." Lillian stopped, afraid to go on.

Winthrop reached out for her hand, but jumped back when there was a noise from the other room.

"Girls? Is that you?" Lillian called. "What are you up to? Come in here, please."

ı she took in their clothing, to which leaves from the bushes where they'd been perched were still attached. "Where exactly have you been?"

Goldie decided it was up to her to take the heat. "I convinced Rose that we needed to be there when the President spoke, Mamma. And we wanted to see you standing up for our rights. You were amazing!"

Lillian was still for a moment, then made her own decision. "I cannot say I am glad you went—it was dangerous and you could have been hurt. However, if you are old enough not to do what I tell you, then you're old enough to live with the consequences. We were all very, very fortunate today."

Shocked, the girls joined their mother and Winthrop Pennington at the table.

"We saw the President choose you to talk to, Mamma, but not much else. We were hiding in the bushes in the back. But why you, Mamma? Why would he want to talk to you?"

Unable to come up with a satisfactory answer, Lillian simply shrugged and changed the subject. "What do think about the President's pledge to coloreds, Winthrop?"

"I think he and the First Lady are sincere. They are the reason I'm considering supporting the NFP. But we all know that sincerity and good intentions only go so far."

Lillian nodded tiredly. Her bed was beckoning. It was time they all hit the hay.

Slowly, she rose from the table and sent the girls, amidst complaints, off to bed. She was about to do the same to Winthrop when he said, "Lillian, I think you should be prepared. The press is likely to be on your doorstep any time now, given the President's interest."

Lillian concentrated on her breathing. She'd never thought of that!

"Well," she said, "It's too late to think about that tonight. I'll see you in the morning, Winthrop."

Winthrop Pennington contemplated Lillian's abrupt change in mood for a while longer before realizing there was no way to understand the female gender. Then he also went to bed.

Chapter 29

It was the next morning, and time for Winthrop to come clean about what he knew. "Lillian, I have something to tell you. Zachary saw his mother in the audience," Winthrop said. "That's why he went off his game."

"I don't understand," Lillian said. "Why would seeing his mother have that effect?"

"No," said Winthrop. "Not his mother. His mother."

Lillian gasped. "You mean to tell me, Winthrop Pennington that you knew all along that the mayor's biological mother was colored? And you kept it from me? You just let me think you didn't know?"

Winthrop hung his head. "I'm so sorry, Lillian. I didn't want to keep the news from you. Even after it was obvious you knew. But I wasn't sure if Carol would be able to make the trip. If she couldn't, then yes, I would have talked with you first."

"It's fine if you didn't trust me with this information, Mr. Pennington, but this situation affects my daughter as well. The mayor will jump to the conclusion that Goldie is the one who told you—or worse. How could you do this without asking my permission? I thought you respected me."

Winthrop blanched. "You're right, Lillian, of course. I...I guess I wasn't thinking. I got caught up in the idea that this time something could really change in this country—that we were finally holding a card that might help our side! Plus, and I know you might not want to hear this, but we've just been getting to know each other. I didn't want to spoil it."

"I still don't understand," Lillian shook her head obstinately.

"You know my immediate family is from Philadelphia, but you don't know that our money was made in New York. My father had a rocky business relationship there with the elder Mr. Stanton, Zach Stanton's father. To put it bluntly, there was a long history of bad blood between them. Stanton swindled my father out of millions. Let's just say that Zachary Stanton the Second may be in the perfect position to pay for the sins of his father."

. . .

It was time to dress for the ball and Lillian's nerves were stretched tighter than a drum.

Winthrop had hatched his plan to "help Zach Stanton become an honest man" by bringing his mother Carol and her brother to town, and now he wanted to get them into the ball. The Blue Landing Club was a private club. She doubted Winthrop could get her in, let alone the three of them. Did Winthrop really believe he had enough clout—and money—to get them all past the sentries?

At least tonight Goldie had promised to stay home with Rose. It seemed Jake was busy with a shipment. Not that Lillian wanted to know anything about that.

She took her gown down off its hanger. Despite her protests, Winthrop had gone ahead and purchased one of the most beautiful dresses Lillian had ever seen. Why, the beadwork alone must have taken a dozen seamstresses many months to finish. There was never any question that she would wear it, so she put her pride aside just this once. The strapless peach-colored fabric with silver beads was simply too lovely to return.

Half an hour later she was ready. Winthrop was waiting for her in his tuxedo, looking for all the world like a sixteen-year-old on his first date. "You look absolutely radiant," he said a little breathlessly.

Goldie and Rose oohed and aahed until the couple was out the door.

"Sure wish we were flies on that wall tonight," said Rose.

"You and me both," said Goldie.

. . .

The four had agreed to meet on the street outside the Blue Landing Club before going into the ball.

"It's a pleasure to meet you," Carol said, holding out her hand. Her voice was raspy, as if from lack of use.

"I am so very sorry for your...loss, Carol," Lillian said.

Carol nodded. "You must be a mother as well, then."

"Yes. Two girls, Goldie and Rose."

"Beautiful names," said Carol. "You are fortunate."

"I surely am," said Lillian.

Carol did not speak for a moment, composing herself. She looked up at the Blue Landing Club. "I suppose y'all are wondering why I'm here after all this time."

"Miss Carol, it's not our place to wonder about that. I assume you want to reconnect with your son."

Elijah, Carol's brother, had accompanied his sister to Aiken. Now he spoke up. "When Mr. Pennington showed up promising to take Carol to see Zachary—well, it was the first time in a very long time that my sister came out of the shell she's been hiding in for all these years. I don't mind saying I was against it, though. I told her to stay put, leave well enough alone. We have a house that's paid for. We have what we need to live and money every month like clockwork to keep up the house." Carol put her hand on his arm. "No, Carol, no, let me have my say." Elijah turned back to Winthrop and Lillian. "But I soon realized that it ain't no way for my sister to live—hidden away like a bad penny. If she needs the world to know that this man is her child, then so be it. And if my nephew wants to take everything from us because the world finds out his secret, then so be it. I love my sister more than I love any house."

Carol's eyes filled with tears, as did Lillian's.

"I must admit to you both," said Winthrop, "that originally my motive in inviting you here was revenge, pure and simple, for the way Zachary Stanton's father cheated mine. But I see there is much, much more at stake than that now."

"Do you think he'll see you?" Lillian asked Carol. "I know how ambitious a man the mayor—your son—is."

"I realize Zachary won't be pleased to see me," Carol said sadly. "But I've wasted too many years of my life longing to see him again. I can't live with this lie anymore. You know how people are. He won't have any choice but to come on home after everyone knows the truth, now will he?"

Lillian foresaw a number of other options, but wisely guarded her tongue.

Winthrop began to outline his plan. "It's very straightforward," he said. "We simply walk in. The public may not care about bad press—in fact, they may even like it in the name of 'protecting their heritage'—but the President is bound to feel otherwise. He cannot afford to be associated with such behavior. His efforts to make the NFP more inclusive could not withstand any whiff of impropriety—such as a colored individual being turned away from an event where he was the guest of honor."

Chapter 30

Goldie had every intention of staying put as she'd promised her mamma. But things being what they were, she had to do what she felt was right.

Jake acted as if he weren't concerned, but Goldie knew him too well. If he thought the Order—including Sheriff Bull Baker—was planning to raid the club, there was only one place Goldie should be: at his side, despite her sister Rose's remonstrations.

. . .

Zachary Stanton considered the many guests filling his club to capacity. He was pleased with the way he'd handled his snafu on the podium, and was certain the President's presence and support would successfully launch his Senate career. He was done with small town politics; he was ready to compete with the big boys. And to do that the first thing on his list was the taking down of one Jake Freeman.

Thoughts of Freeman immediately brought Goldie Jackson to mind. She hadn't appeared at work since Stanton's admission. But he was hopeful that after the President left and things died down, she'd see the light and agree to go with him to Washington. After all, what kind of life did she have here in Aiken? Spending the rest of her days as the girlfriend of a rumrunner?

He watched the President and First Lady pose for photo after photo in the expectation they were establishing a new image for the National Federal Party, one that was moving away from that good ol' boy image and into a future of inclusivity. The President's wife, however, looked distracted, constantly searching out her husband's arm and eye. The President appeared not to notice. Something was definitely going on between the two. Stanton chalked it up to the state of marriage. Look at his own, for example. Plenty of ups and downs there.

The local guests were busy angling for an audience with the President, as if being in his presence even for a moment would change the very nature of their existence. Of course, various presidents had visited Aiken before, but had never allowed access to such a personal degree, and this type of exposure could bring significant business to their fair city. If the presidential couple left with a positive sense of Aiken, they would tell their friends. It was not out of the realm of possibility that a new tradition of visiting presidents could be starting this very night.

As for the help, Stanton watched as they vied in the same way for the honor of serving the President. While it was always a treat to serve any president, President Jameson was the first one to address their issues directly—and the only one to invite a colored woman to enter into a conversation. And do it in private!

Zach looked at his watch. At some point shortly he would have to check on the sheriff to see how the sting operation was going. He'd trusted the sheriff in the past, at least to get the job done, but that trust had flown out the window when coloreds had strolled onto the grounds—Stanton's grounds!—and disrupted his rally.

Where was Bull's man, anyway? The sheriff was supposed to send someone to keep Zach informed.

Zachary quickly summoned Mr. Edmond, the head server. "What's holding up the delivery? They should have been here by now."

"Yes, sir. We almost out of champagne. I'll come for you soon as word comes they're on the way."

Zachary's eyes followed the action in the room. Harpists, violinists, and pianists were playing, tactfully quiet. The guests' glasses were filled as soon as they emptied. Mr. Edmond angled up to Zach's side just as he was about to refill his own.

"Sir, we have a situation at the foyer."

"A situation?"

"I think it's best you go handle it, sir," Mr. Edmond said quietly.

Annoyed, Zachary moved to the foyer, where two individuals were standing.

Lillian! Zach felt faint from the sight of her in a gown of a million stars.

Then he saw who was standing next to her. Pennington. That bastard.

Now Zachary was confused. What was Pennington doing there with Lillian? And who were those colored people with them? The woman looked like—

Zach recoiled, recovering just enough to keep from stumbling. He had to get them out of there, whoever they were!

The reporters and photographers were faster, however. Zach halted, unsure and shaking. He had to think fast. Make the most of a bad situation. Act as if...as if what?

Pennington was returning Zach's look with a checkmate glare.

Everyone was waiting for the mayor to react. To do something. He felt the President and First Lady at his back. Very quietly, Zach spoke to Pennington. "Pennington. I should have known."

"Mayor."

"I'd leave right now," said Zach, "if you know what's good for you.

"If you're referring to my gorgeous guest here—"

"Pennington, let's not make this situation any uglier than it has to be. You know she—they—cannot be here."

"From what I understand," said Pennington, holding tightly to his date's arm, "as my guest she has every right to be here."

The sheriff and four Secret Service agents had joined them in the foyer.

"Is there a problem, Mayor?" asked the President.

"No, no problem, Mr. President. It seems Mr. Pennington here is confused about our membership policy. I was merely setting him straight."

"Oh?" asked the First Lady. "And what exactly is your policy?"

Zach felt the sweat pool in his armpits and stream down his brow. "With all due respect, Mrs. Jameson, you must know that the Blue Landing Club does not allow coloreds. And since she is not a member of the club, well...."

The First Lady responded wryly. "Why, Mr. Mayor, that seems like an odd ruling tonight of all nights, given the fact that so many here are not members of your club. And when you put it like that, even the President and I are here as guests. Aren't we, dear?"

"So we are," said the President. He turned to Zach. "My wife is right," he said under his breath. "This is an NFP-sponsored event. We need and want Mr. Pennington's support as well as his family's. Are you prepared to sabotage our chances?"

Aloud, he said, "Well, Mr. Mayor, I'm sure we can find a way to make an exception for the benefit of all this one night, no?"

Zachary struggled for composure. "Yes, of course. Absolutely, Mr. President. I suppose an exception can be made for this most special night." He turned to Lillian. "Mrs. Jackson, won't you join us in the Blue Landing Club?"

. . .

That did it for Bull.

With the entrance of the activist Winthrop Pennington and Lillian Jackson and the other colored couple with them, the last vestige of the sheriff's patience was snuffed out. Stanton was done for.

. . .

Winthrop's first stop was the President and the First Lady.

"Don't let's be shy, then," Lillian hissed in his ear.

Winthrop only grinned.

"Good evening Mr. President, Mrs. Jameson. May I present Lillian Jackson?"

"What a lovely gown, Miss Jackson," said the First Lady, feeling instinctively that if circumstances were different this woman and she could be friends. How many women would be courageous enough to take on the whole white world of Aiken, South Carolina like this?

Lillian demurely thanked the First Lady, feeling timid, an emotion she had felt very few times in her life. At the same time she was still marveling at the fact that she and the mayor's mother and her brother had actually made it through the front door.

President Jameson chuckled and shook his head, purposefully avoiding Lillian's gaze. "You're exactly what we need at this party, Winthrop...shake things up a little. I hope you're seriously considering making that change to the NFP?"

"I'm considering it, sir."

"I assume you'll give your father a firsthand account of this weekend's events."

In other words: Make sure to tell your father that the President and the NFP conducted themselves spectacularly. "I certainly intend to, sir," said Winthrop.

. . .

It was killing Zach not to be included in the little tête à tête going on in the ballroom. Did Lillian Jackson's presence mean that Goldie had told her mother about his past—about his mother? Had Lillian told Pennington? Would Pennington tell the President?

Suddenly, Mr. Edmond was again at his side. The man was a damn ghost, spooking him all the time. The mayor was informed it was time to take delivery on the "goods." Mr. Edmond liked to talk in code.

Speaking of ghosts, as he turned, Zachary could have sworn he saw his mother once again. But it was simply impossible. Not here! Not in a ball gown! It must be some other woman, someone with skin just dark enough to cause her to resemble the woman he'd barely known and cast aside. Some friend of Lillian's or. . . .

He looked around for Bull, but couldn't find him. He was not surprised; Bull had been a major disappointment on the dependability front. He located Sheriff Moody and tapped him on the shoulder, gesturing with his thumb that it was time to go.

Zachary explained to the sheriff that he would be providing the backup for the liquor delivery. He also told Sheriff Moody that after the workers of the Blue Landing Club left the area with the club's liquor, the feds were scheduled to bust Jake Freemen.

Sheriff Moody grinned. He was looking forward to meeting this notorious character he had heard so much about. Then he had a thought.

"Hold on a minute there, Mayor. Where's Sheriff Baker? I wouldn't want to step on any toes."

The mayor was dismissive. "I'll handle him if he gives you any trouble."

Sheriff Moody nodded. No skin off his nose.

They left the Blue Landing Club heading south on Whiskey Road to an area prime for an upgrade. To Stanton, it was only a matter of time before costly estates lined the wide, tree-shaded road.

When they arrived, Bull was there along with three Blue Landing Club workers and a truck. The two men got out of Zachary's car and approached. Zachary noted Bull's expression. Obviously, he was none too pleased to see Sheriff Moody on the scene, not that it mattered.

"Sheriff," he said, letting his irritation show. "Fancy meeting you here."

"Just staying on top of things like you asked me to."

Bull was two steps ahead of the mayor, neglecting to inform him that there were reporters ready to capture the liquor marshals as they took down Jake Freeman. Only now, due to an "anonymous" tip, the take-down would include one Zachary Stanton, Jr. Several Order members were hidden in the bushes, ready to go to battle at the crook of Bull's finger.

Stanton rolled his eyes. The delivery should have been completed by now. What was holding them up? His trucks should be long gone before Freeman arrived for his delivery. "I don't have time for this delay tonight. In case you haven't noticed, I have the President of the United States at my club waiting on me to return with some of the finest libations money can buy."

When Bull rocked back on his heels without answering, Stanton sneered. "I will be so relieved when I don't have to deal with this small town bullshit anymore."

Zach spent the next several minutes while they waited for the distributors to show up debating with himself. Had he actually seen his mother at the ball...or was he experiencing some kind of breakdown, perhaps from all the pressure of the President's visit and his own impending run for the U.S. Senate? But who was he kidding? He wouldn't exactly say he was wracked with guilt for having such a minimal relationship with his biological mother. His life had been pretty sweet, all in all, and frankly, he hadn't missed her. Yet, for whatever reason, the twinges of regret had been increasing, like persistent, annoying taps of a bird on a window pane.

On the other hand, wouldn't someone have noticed her presence as well? What about his eagle-eyed wife? One colored woman on the arm of a white man at the ball was disruptive enough, but two colored women? Or would the guests have dismissed her as a servant? Zach wished he smoked cigarettes. And had a tall tumbler of whiskey in his hand.

. . .

A moment later, Jake Freeman began to approach with a few of his men, but paused, staying out of sight. He paused when he saw the mayor—and not one but two sheriffs. Something was up.

. . .

Curt Armbrister had a reputation of his own, having grown rich off the back of the illegal rum trade. His organization was such that he no longer had to make the runs to folks like the Blue Landing Club anymore, but he loved the thrill of it. Wouldn't trade it for anything in the world, in fact. And, despite the inevitability of any repeal, he intended to continue selling a cheaper version of whatever product would capture the market. But there were too many people in the clearing for his taste when he arrived.

"Bull, who the hell is this character in the monkey suit?" he asked with a snarl.

"I'm the man who made you rich," said the mayor pompously. "I am the owner of the Blue Landing Club."

"Humph," spat Armbrister. "Let's get one thang straight, then, owner of the Blue Landing Club. You ain't no more made me rich than I made you wealthy."

Zachary reappraised the man before him. "Touché," he said.

"You listen here, Bull," Armbrister warned. "I can't be doing business with someone be talkin' crazy shit."

The mayor puffed up with hauteur. "Let's just say we've made each other a lot of money and leave it at that," he said.

"Yeah, well, I s'pose," said Armbrister, unconvinced but eager to finish off the transaction. "But where's Jake? It's him supposed to be here, not you."

"There's been a change in plans," said the mayor. "I'll be taking delivery on my packages first, then Freeman."

"Really," said Armbrister. "That so? You know what, Mr. Highfalutin'? You 'bout to make me cut y'all off. I don't have time for raggedy business dealings."

"Tell you what, then," said Zachary. "Let's finish up here and then we'll call it quits. I think the club could stand to go dry for a few months until the law is repealed."

"Fine by me," said Carl. "You ain't my biggest buyer anyway. Now, if Jake Freeman wanted out, that'd be another story."

Armbrister instructed his men to load the mayor's truck. While they were shifting box after box from one truck to the other, Zachary took out his payment.

A loud rumble emanated from the direction of the woods. Armbrister stopped, his hand outstretched. "Shit, what was that?"

Bull assumed it was the liquor marshals. But then, out stepped Charlie Stevens, the supreme leader of the Order, holding Goldie, struggling like a demented cat, in his arms.

"What the hell's goin' on here?" demanded Armbrister, glaring at the mayor and drawing his gun. His men did the same. "I don't like bein' jerked around."

"Yeah, what the hell's goin' on, here, Bull?" demanded the mayor.

"Looks to me like this lil' lady been pokin' her nose into grown folk business," said Stevens.

Zachary was shaking. "Take your hands off her. That's not necessary. She likely got turned around on her way home or something. Woman's not too smart, I hear."

It was a yarn, and Zachary knew it. Unfortunately, so did just about every other person there. They all knew the Jackson girls—and their reputation for being smart as whips.

. . .

Jake Freeman had stepped into the clearing. Now he froze. The sight of Charlie Stevens with his nasty white hands on his beloved Goldie was more than an insult. It was downright wrong. The men on each side of him each grabbed a shoulder to restrain him. "Wait a minute, boss. Don't do anything stupid. See what happens. They might let her go."

"She ain't that stupid," said Charlie Stevens, who had turned when he heard Jake and his men approach. "She know she ain't supposed to let the sun go down on her on the south side. I think her boyfriend there sent her over here to spy, that's what I think."

Zachary opened his mouth to speak. At that moment, Jake broke free. "Let her go right now, Stevens, or I'll blow your fucking head off." He pulled a handgun out of his waistband and leveled it at Charlie.

Bull saw his perfect plan spiraling out of control.

Jake cocked his gun. "I said, take your filthy hands off her. Right. Now."

But Charlie Stevens wasn't ready to comply. "She wants to play with the big boys? I say, let her. She kinda cute for a nigga gal, too."

Jake heard the threat for what it was—an attempt to make him lose his cool—but reacted anyway. He charged at Stevens.

Several men appeared out of the darkness, weapons raised. Zachary and Bull grabbed Jake before he got to Stevens and Goldie. Zachary, because he still had feelings for her, and Bull because he needed to appear innocent to the liquor marshals, who didn't want to blow the bust or have the blood of an innocent girl on their hands.

"Freeze! U.S. Marshals! Drop your guns!" Four agents flashed their badges.

"Agent William Dent, U.S. liquor marshal," said one. "No one needs to get hurt. Now drop your weapons."

Nary a man made a move.

"Gentlemen, you have been issued an order by a United States liquor marshal. Failure to obey will result in a plethora of federal charges—or worse," Agent Dent warned. He shouldered a couple of his agents into position around the small group of men.

"I ain't tellin' my men to put down shit," yelled Jake, "until he lets Goldie go!" He was attempting to pry his arm from Bull's iron grip without success.

"Sir, I assure you nothing will happen to the young lady. We need you to tell your men to put down their weapons."

"Like I said, not until they let her go and drop theirs."

"Mr. Freeman, I insist. We need you to do what we say."

How did the liquor marshal know his name? And why would Jake be the only one who should drop his gun? Things were looking more and more like a setup.

"No. Let her go first."

It was a stand-off.

Until Andrew Little, never a patient Order devotee, grew tired of the back and forth and fired his weapon.

Chapter 31

All hell broke loose.

Zachary and Bull let Jake go at the same time so they could take cover. Jake aimed straight for Charlie Stevens.

The Order took that as the signal, letting go with a haze of bullets. Jake's men had his back, but they were grossly outnumbered by the Order, the marshals, and the rumrunner's men.

Curt Armbrister slipped out of the way quicker than an eel. This was a personal fight, and he wanted no part of it. If they were after his liquor, that would have been another story, but since they were not, he was not prepared to take a bullet—or go to the slammer—for any of them.

The Order had it in for Jake, but showed little concern about where their bullets might land. On their part, the marshals were almost equally unrestrained in their defense. One of their bullets hit Charlie Stevens in the head. As he toppled to the ground, Goldie fell away in a swoon.

It was dark and the air was full of smoke. She couldn't make out anything but the seemingly endless flashes of gunpowder. She cried out for Jake and rolled behind a bush, shielding her head with her hands.

Then there was silence.

. . .

When the acrid smoke cleared, Goldie garnered the courage to peer through the fingers of her hands. The moon's glow revealed a number of bodies on the ground. She scanned each one frantically, trying to identify them. Where was Jake?

Then she saw him, arms and legs akimbo. She ran to his side, screaming his name. But it was too late. Even through all the blood, she could see he'd taken bullets in his heart, neck, and stomach.

"My love," he whispered softly, coughing. "You fool woman. You . . . followed . . . me."

"Jake, I'm sorry. I'm so sorry. I had to make sure you were all right. Please don't be mad at me," Goldie sobbed.

"I could never . . . stay mad . . . at you. I love you, Goldie." Jake turned away as blood flowed from his mouth.

"Jake, don't leave me. You'll be fine. The ambulance will be here soon. We'll be together, I promise."

"No...least not...on this earth. Keep...that heart...of gold, you hear, sweet love?" he said.

Then he was gone.

. . .

The mayor slid out from behind the tree where he'd run for cover. He slowly went across the street to help Goldie up. She collapsed into his arms. The federal agents were already rounding up what was left of the Order, and Goldie's presence, he felt, would not be missed.

Jake Freeman was dead, but Isaac, Jake's right hand man, had survived, and he still considered himself Goldie's protector.

"Take yo' dirty hands off her, Mayor."

"I...I was...."

"Don't much care what you was doin'. She ain't one o' yours. Now, back off."

Zachary lurched away. Suddenly, the magnitude of the night's events hit him in the gut. He, Mayor Zachary Stanton, the President's choice for a senate position, had been involved in a shootout. With rumrunners, federal agents, and members of the WWO. His career was likely over.

Unless he pulled himself together.

He had to formulate a plan. Act the part of an injured public official, beleaguered by forces beyond his control. He approached the marshal.

"Agent Dent, thank God you're all right. It's a good thing you were here. Don't know what I would have done.... Now you know the extent of what I've been dealing with down here. That Jake Freeman was one tough character."

Agent Dent looked Zach squarely in the eye. "There was significant loss of life here tonight, Mayor. We will need to conduct an investigation. If I may, I'll start with a few questions for you."

"Yes, yes, of course," Zachary said as if he wanted nothing more than to be of service. "But I assume we can do this another time, Marshall? The President is waiting for me."

Zachary squirmed under Agent Dent's stare, hoping the use of his connection with the President would sway the man's instincts.

"Tomorrow morning, then," the marshall finally said.

"Certainly. Tomorrow," agreed Zachary. "At my estate."

. . .

Sheriff Bull Baker was left, as usual, to clean up the mess. He spent the next four hours answering questions, and even then the feds said they would have to talk to him again in the morning.

First order would be the Order, naturally, and their involvement where they hadn't been invited. Bull for one would not mourn the passing of Andrew Little, always too hotheaded for his own good and that of his fellow members. But when Bull spotted Johnathon Appleton, the Order's voice of reason, lying in the dirt, he'd felt bile rise in his throat.

The mayor, that little weasel, had skedaddled quick as his legs could carry him. The sheriff had other things to think about, though. Such as how in the heck he could explain the WWO's presence. He'd have to stick to his usual line: that the Order were nothing but a law-abiding group of white men concerned with the safety of their city and that tonight that meant stopping Jake Freeman once and for all.

The man comforting Goldie—one of Freeman's men—was speaking with a reporter who'd been on the scene when the whole nightmare unfolded. Agent Dent approached them, dismissing the reporter who left, but not without a lot of grumbling. Then the agent eyeballed the sheriff and the other WWO members like a search beacon homing in on its target. Bull didn't bother to tell him that anything the WWO said was likely to be nothing more than propaganda. He'd have to figure that out for himself.

Goldie insisted on knowing who had shot Jake. Although Agent Dent assured her he would let them know what they found out, Goldie and Isaac found his reassurances hollow. Agent Dent did, however, inform Isaac that he had to go with the agents for questioning and then instructed another agent to escort Goldie safely home.

Chapter 32

Lillian and Winthrop, blind, or so it seemed, to the ogling and comments of the guests at the ball, danced the night away. Then the President tapped Winthrop on the shoulder. "May I have this dance?" he asked.

Lillian wasn't sure if she imagined the loud gasp from the onlookers. She looked at Winthrop for a cue.

"Of course, Mr. President," he said. "Perhaps I might have the honor with your lovely wife?"

The President bowed his agreement, and Lillian was left alone with the man for whom she had pined these many long years since her earliest memories.

There was no time for chit-chat, personal or otherwise, however, because just then the mayor returned, looking a lot worse for wear.

There was an instant hush while the room took in his disheveled appearance.

Immediately aware of the reaction of his guests, Zachary looked down and then quickly straightened his tie and tucked in his shirt, pasting what barely passed as a smile on his face. When the guests saw the mayor did not plan to share the nature of his apparent misadventure, they slowly, and with obvious disappointment, renewed their drinking and conversations, but continued to send periodic glances his way.

Zachary poured himself a stiff drink to calm his nerves. Everything would be fine. He had the President's endorsement. Jake Freeman was dead. No one except Bull knew the extent of the mayor's involvement, and the sheriff knew his own ass was on the line if he experienced an attack of loose lips. Zach refilled his glass and stepped onto the terrace.

"Mr. Mayor," a voice said.

"Oh! Mrs. Jameson. You startled me."

"Please, call me Claire."

"Claire, then," Zach said uncomfortably. "I hope you're having a good time tonight."

"Certainly," said the First Lady. "And I've been to many soirees, as you can imagine."

Zach nodded. He didn't have the patience for mental games right now.

"I've met people from every corner of the world, Mayor. And, do you know what?"

Where was this headed?

"Nearly all of them want to be my husband. Hence, the whole reason we are here this weekend."

"Mrs.—Claire, I have to win the Senate before I can even dream about the presidency."

"Nonsense!" said the First Lady. "That didn't stop my husband, and it won't stop you."

. . .

Liam saw his chance when it was clear his wife was engrossed in a conversation with the mayor—who, it seemed, had something to hide. But right now, there were more important matters to attend to.

"Elle. My Elle. Here in my arms once again."

"Liam! Don't talk like that. Anyone could hear!" Lillian whispered.

"Elle, we have to talk."

"What? No! That's impossible."

"Tell Pennington you're tired. Meet me at your place. I won't take no for an answer, Elle."

Lillian looked away, but did not say no.

"We deserve this, Elle. I deserve some answers about what happened all those years ago. I never stopped thinking about you. Now, say you'll meet me before I cause a scene. We can have this conversation here, now, or at your house. It's up to you."

Lillian sighed. Liam always was stubborn. This time he might do something foolhardy.

"All right," she whispered. "I'll go tell Winthrop I'm leaving. I'll come up with something."

Five minutes later, a stretch limousine was waiting for Lillian at the foot of the club's steps. The door swung open and she climbed in. As they slowly pulled down the gravel driveway onto Whiskey Road toward Easy Street, Liam gently put his hand on Lillian's, but neither spoke a word.

Lillian whispered, "How does he know where to go?"

"Elle, I'm the President. I have access to anything I want to know. And right now I want to get to know you all over again."

Lillian flushed with pleasure.

When they arrived at the Jackson residence, a second limo pulled up behind them. "My detail. They stay with me at all times."

Lillian nodded. The life of a president was new to her.

"Gentleman, wait out here on the porch. I'll be fine."

"But sir, we need to check the house and the perimeter first."

"I insist. And that's an order," said the President.

The agents didn't like it, but followed their commander's directive. One agent stood at the front door and the other walked toward the backyard and stood catty corner to the back porch, where he could see both the porch and front yard.

Lillian gingerly closed the door behind them. "We need to be quiet. My girls are sleeping."

"Your girls? How many do you have?"

"Two. Goldie and Rose."

The questions in Liam's eyes caused Lillian to look down at the floor. "Have a seat while I check on them," she said. "I'll be right back."

But when Lillian opened the door to the kitchen, Goldie ran to her mother's bosom. Lillian could comprehend nothing except Jake's name.

"What is it, Goldie? Did something happen to Jake? Tell me. I can't help you unless I can understand you."

Rose spoke up, understanding that Goldie's hysterics were not going to pass any time soon.

"Mamma, Jake's dead. They murdered him...just like Daddy!"

"Say what? Jake? What are you talking about?"

Goldie let out another wail and pressed even closer to her mother's breast.

An image came to Lillian's mind, that of Zachary Stanton, Mayor of Aiken, stumbling into his own ball looking as if he'd been in a brawl. There was no doubt in her mind that he was involved in Jake's killing.

It took a while, but when Goldie calmed enough to speak, Lillian learned how her daughter had again disobeyed and gone out to "protect" her man. This second brush with death was more than Lillian could take in.

"You followed him?" she asked tiredly. "Lord, what came over you?"

Goldie hiccupped a few times. "I knew Mayor Stanton and Sheriff Bull were planning something. And I was right."

"And just what did you think you were going to do about it?"

"I don't know. I thought I could warn Jake or something. But now...now he's dead, Mamma, he's d...d...dead!"

At that moment, Lillian remembered she had the President of the United States in her living room waiting to "discuss" their situation. The world had been turned upside down for sure. She comforted Goldie as best she could and told the girls to wait there and she would be back shortly.

Liam was indeed waiting on the sofa for her, not too patiently either, it seemed. He stood up quickly.

"Elle, I know what happened to your husband. I am so sorry." He reached for her, but she held back, glancing over her shoulder.

"Did you love him? Were you happy?" Liam asked in quick succession. "Did you ever think about me?"

"Liam, please, one question at a time. Yes, I loved him, probably about as much as you love your wife."

"But what happened? Why did you leave? Why did you come here?"

"Do you have to ask, Liam? You're not stupid. This story has been played out since time immemorial."

Liam nodded, downcast. "I suppose so," he finally said. "Not for sure, of course, but deep down in my gut. My family had aspirations for me. They thought you would get in the way of all that. It was no secret how I felt about you, Elle."

"Liam. Really! You can't possibly think they bothered to send me away because of your 'feelings' for me." She looked away, shaking her head.

Liam was shocked. "Whatever do you mean?"

"Think, Liam! Why would a white family send away the lover of their adored son?"

Slowly a look of realization passed over Liam's face.

"Oh, my God. You were pregnant! With my child!"

Lillian nodded.

"But why didn't you tell me? I had a right to know, Elle."

"I didn't get the chance, Liam. As soon as my mother found out, they packed me up and shipped me out."

"Again, why? There were other mixed children being raised on the property. You know my family would've done right by you."

Again Lillian shook her head at his sheltered perspective. "My family knew that the baby would be seen as a threat to your future. And they were right to take me away! Look at you—President of the United States of America. Do you think you'd be where you are now if I had stayed to raise our daughter with you?"

"Daughter, did you say daughter?" Liam had tears in his eyes. "Elle, are you telling me that your older daughter is mine?"

"Yes, Liam, that's exactly what I'm saying."

"Goldie, right? It's a beautiful name. But that settles it. I cannot and will not live the rest of my life without you and our daughter."

"That's nonsense, Liam," Lillian said, hands on her hips. "Goldie has no idea Denver Jackson was not her biological father. And I do not intend to tell her."

"But, Lillian. I need you both in my life. Life is too short. That's something you know better than anyone."

"That's not fair, Liam. Don't use Denver's death to win my commitment. It's beneath you."

Liam appeared appropriately chastised. "I'm just saying we've wasted too much time as it is. That we've been given a second chance, Elle. Let's take it. Lillian, are you going to make me the happiest man alive and marry me?"

Apparently, William Jameson, the current President of the United States of America, did not see his married status as a deterrent.

"I…." Lillian could not tear her eyes from the man she had loved since they had shared everything from grits to giggling with delight as they played endless games of hide-and-seek on the vast plantation.

And then, later, passion.

But it was not to be. Lillian prayed to God for strength. She would need it for the words she had to speak.

"I love you, Liam, I always have. Denver was my husband, and I loved him dearly, but you and I…we were different. You know that. But there is too much at stake."

How she wanted to jump right into Liam's arms and stay there forever! But they were not living in utopia. This was the 1930s and a colored mistress, let alone a colored wife, if such a thing could even be imagined, in the White House was not something people were prepared to accept.

"You think you will have supporters after you send the First Lady away and replace her with me and my two girls? A colored woman and her colored children? In the White House?"

"I will divorce Claire quietly," Liam scrambled. "Well, it won't be quiet, that can't be helped, but I'll do it. I won't run for a second term."

"Listen to yourself, Liam. You must stop this nonsense. You have important work to do. People are depending on you. This country is depending on you."

"But I love you, Elle. I always have."

"I love you, too, Liam, even after all these years. But we have to do what's best for the country."

Liam looked at her so bleakly that Lillian nearly capitulated. Then she tried to picture herself and the girls in the White House and the image got fuzzy. "No, Liam. This—we—has to end. I…I have to ask you to leave."

. . .

The President aged in front of her eyes. She could see he knew she was right.

The door to the kitchen swung open.

"Goldie, is that you?" asked Lillian. "Get back to your room. I'll be there directly."

"It's not Goldie, Lillian—or should I say 'Elle'? It's me. Pitney."

Pitney!

Lillian's remorse hit her hard and strong. In the last couple of weeks Pitney had fallen out of her life like a distant memory. Lillian had wondered a time or two why Pitney had made herself so scarce, but with Winthrop and Liam and her entire past history brought to the surface, it was as if her life with Pitney, the woman whose friendship she had cherished, had never existed. How could she have been so cruel?

Lillian ran over to her. "Pitney! I haven't seen you in so long. But what are you doing here so late. That's all right. Come in, come in. I'd like you to meet—"

"Stop it, Lillian. Just stop. How could you do it? I heard you talking. You're planning to leave Aiken, aren't you?"

"No, Pitney, no. I'm not leaving Aiken. You misunderstood—"

"I understand completely, Lillian. You don't have to lie to me."

"Pitney, stop. I would never lie to you. I care about you. The girls care about you. What do you think you—"

The President felt it was time he made his exit. The situation could quickly degenerate and a scandal would gum up the works on all fronts. "Um, excuse me," he said, "but I'm afraid I must be going."

"Stop right there." Pitney reached behind her back. Suddenly a gun was in her hand. She raised it slowly.

"Oh my God," Lillian breathed. "Liam, go! Pitney. What are you doing? Why are you doing this?"

"Stay away from him, Lillian. You don't need him. You have everything you could ever need right here with me."

The President heard the voice of unrequited love and pitied Pitney. Whoever she was, he understood her pain.

"Pit, stop," pleaded Lillian. "This isn't like you. Why don't you give me that gun? You don't want to hurt anybody. You fight enough at home. This ain't you."

Pitney appeared to soften, but only for a moment. Then she squeezed off a shot into the wall. "Don't you come near me, Lillian. You're the reason I'm in this mess. You think you can use people just because you get lonely?"

The shot alerted the Secret Service, who burst through the front and the back doors, guns drawn.

Two seconds later, Sheriff Bull Baker followed. "What in tarnation is goin' on here?"

"Sheriff, we got it covered," said one of the agents. "We need you to step back. Mr. President, it's time to go."

The President took a willing step toward the door.

"I said, don't move!" screamed Pitney.

Bull moved in. "Maybe I can help," he said to the agent. "I know these people. They coloreds, but they ain't no trouble. They ain't gone hurt the President." He looked at Pitney, but sidestepped toward the President to get between him and Lillian Jackson. "Come on, Pitney, you know you've never hurt anyone in your life. It's time to set the gun down. Nothin'll happen to you if you put the gun down now."

"What are you gone do?" Pitney cried. Her hand was shaking with the effort of keeping the revolver up and pointed.

"I'm not gone do nothing, Pitney," promised the sheriff quietly. "I just want everybody to be safe, that's all. You see these men here.

They're here to protect the President. They're likely to shoot you if you don't put that gun away real quick. You don't want to leave your kids with that mean sonovabitch husband of yours. Do you?"

Tears ravaged Pitney's face. The trembling in her hand increased.

"Bull, I don't think you're helping," whispered Lillian.

"What you care about my kids? You just as mean as he is. Lillian leaves I'll have no one. There are only so many chances in this life to find love." Pitney's attention shifted back to Lillian. "You forgot all about me, didn't you? What with all your finery, your white man, and your President."

"No, Pit, no, I would never forget about you," said Lillian, but it was lie and they both knew it. She had forgotten.

Bull saw something in Pitney's eyes that he'd seen in plenty of men's eyes before. The look that said she didn't care if she lived or died. As her hand tightened on the trigger, he was already drawing his weapon, pushing Lillian out of the way, and stepping in front of the President.

. . .

When it was over, Bull Baker was lying on the floor. The President and his Secret Service agents had fled. Lillian walked on her knees to Bull's side. "Sheriff. Bull. Are you okay? Bull, you're going to be all right. And just so you know, I'm not nearly done being angry with you. Why'd you have to go be a hero on account of me?"

"Miss Lillian…." Bull had trouble speaking. "I…I couldn't let anything happen to you, too. I always regretted what happened to Denver. He was a good man, colored or not, and I let him down."

"Calm yourself, Bull. Save your strength." Lillian looked around for something to tie off Bull's shoulder wound. Her petticoat would have to do. She ripped off a long piece and wrapped his arm carefully. He was losing blood, but the wound didn't appear life-threatening.

Lillian felt a hand on her shoulder. It was Liam.

"What are you doing here, Liam? I thought you left. Go on, git out of here!"

"Lillian, the ambulance is coming for both of them."

The President took one more long searching look of Lillian's face before sprinting out the back door.

Did he say "both of them"?

Lillian turned. Sure enough, Pitney was also lying on the floor between the kitchen and the living room, her eyes wide open and empty.

Chapter 33

It took Shelby a moment or two to find her tongue.

"You mean to tell me the sheriff took a bullet for Grandmamma?"

"Just proves that people are never all good or all bad, Shelby. The sheriff's nature was always warring in the man. This time, he made a change. Quit the Order altogether, upheld the law as best he could. Our families became friends—least as friendly as blacks and whites could be in those days. It took a while for Laney to come on board, but Bull persisted."

"What happened to the mayor?"

"After the headlines came out—'Colored Gangster Mayor Involved in Shootout,' I believe one read—his humiliation was complete. He tried to explain himself to the President, of course, but it was too late. President Jameson wouldn't even grant him an audience. Zachary Stanton's career was officially over."

It was all there in black and white, so to speak. Zachary Stanton's heritage in ink for everyone to see. He was asked to withdraw from the Senate race and the President's announcement of Stanton's candidacy for Senator of South Carolina was no longer supported.

"Bull Baker was elected mayor?"

"He sure was," said Goldie. "And a darn sight better one he made than the last one."

"His wife left him, too," said Rose. "Caroline never was fond of the south, and being married to a passing colored man was not the way she wanted to be remembered. She moved back to New York and filed for divorce. Zachary, poor thing, remained in Aiken to run the Blue Landing Club. By the end of 1933, Prohibition was overturned, just as President Jameson promised. The club began to operate legally and slowly regained its luster, but it never quite reached the same status or hosted such elite clientele."

"But, what about Grandmamma and the President?" asked Shelby. "Didn't they ever get a chance to—"

"Are you ladies ever coming back to this party or what?"

Uncle Rich appeared at the door. "Come on, now, we're all waitin'. There's a big old birthday cake downstairs just waiting to be eaten. Goldie? Rose? Come on, now, Shelby. For heaven's sake, girl, you're hosting this event!"

"You gotta be kidding me," Shelby groaned.

Uncle Rich looked put out.

"Oh, I'm sorry, Uncle Rich. I didn't mean you. We'll be right there, I promise. Go on back down. We'll join you in a minute."

Uncle Rich left unwillingly, shaking his head and mumbling something about those "darn women and their yacking."

Shelby turned to her mother. "So? What happened, Mamma? Tell me the rest! Did Grandmamma and the President see each other again?"

"There's not all that much to tell," said Goldie, shaking her head. "There never was a need for them to be in each other's presence again. They both knew that the President's career would be finished if word got out of any impropriety. They spoke occasionally, of course, and agreed that he would stay in his marriage until he finished office. Of course, then he was reelected to a second term."

"And then did they get together?" Shelby pushed.

"Yes and no," Rose said. "He did divorce Claire—as quietly as possible—when he left office. After that, he joined Grandmamma. They had one good year together before he passed away from a heart attack."

"Well, that is about the saddest story I've ever heard," said Shelby.

"No," said Goldie. "You musn't feel bad for our Lillian. She found love—twice. Some people never find it once."

"But that means you didn't ever really get to know him, your real father, I mean."

"Denver Jackson was my 'real' father," said Goldie sternly. "Still, I wanted to know this man who had loved my mother for so long. When I graduated college he was just finishing his term at the White House. By then, I was building a life for us. Although he was very generous, paid for both of our educations, Rose's and mine."

"He was a good man," agreed Rose, "a good, good man."

There was a long silence while the three women pondered the ways that life twisted and turned. Then Goldie said to her daughter, "I said I was going home, Shelby, but I didn't mean to Aiken. I meant to our home in Virginia."

Shelby's eyes lit up.

"That's right. The President willed his family estate to me, the same one I will be passing on to you and your children someday. In the meantime, I want to see you all enjoy it while I'm still around to share in the fun."

Goldie held out her arms and enveloped Shelby in a big hug. "Young lady, it's time for a road trip!"

About the Author

Shi Evans is a program assistant in the Georgetown area of Washington, D.C. with a degree in political science and an MPA. Shi started writing after working with the FBI and living in South Korea on military orders. With almost twenty years as a military spouse, she has logged a vast number of travel miles and met the most interesting characters from all over the world. She taps into these experiences to bring forth her first novel, Whiskey Road.

Made in the USA
Charleston, SC
09 December 2014